Between
Heaven and Hell

Raymond D. Mason

Between Heaven and Hell
(The Sackett Series – Book #6)

Copyright © 2013 by Raymond D. Mason
Published by Raymond D. Mason
For Kindle E-Books

You may order paperback books through:
www.Amazon.com
www.BarnesandNoble.com
Borders.com
www.CreateSpace.com
www.Target.com

Or, personalized autograph copies from
The Author at
RMason3092@aol.com

This is a work of fiction. All characters, names, incidents, organizations, and dialogue in this novel are either the products of the author's imagination or are used fictitiously.

Book Edited by Lance Knight
For Editing Services contact Mr. Knight at
muser4u@gmail.com

Note: If you order paperbacks from <u>Create Space</u> use the <u>discount code L9ZJ9ZJJ</u> for a <u>30% discount</u>.

Preface

BRENT SACKETT was all right with being a man on the dodge until he met a woman; Julia Summers. The one time deputy sheriff had crossed over the line when he was a member of a posse that cornered a man who had robbed a freight office in Crystal City, Texas.

When Brent was told to circle around the rock formation where the bandit had held up he shot and killed the man. With no one having seen him, Brent hid the money the man had stolen with the intention of returning later and picking it up for himself.

When the sheriff figured out what Brent was up to he followed him and caught him in the act of retrieving the loot. In the sheriff's attempt to arrest Brent, Sackett shot and killed him, thereby putting him on the run.

During his flight from the law, however, Brent met a woman who began to make him see the error of his ways and wanting to start a new life with her as his wife.

Brian Sackett, Brent's identical twin brother, had returned to the Sackett ranch after the War Between the States and along with his oldest brother AJ, was running the ranch owned by their father, John Sackett.

When AJ was shot and seriously wounded by one of the Sackett's hired hands, Brian struck out on the trail of the man believed to be responsible. His trail led him through parts of Texas where Brent had committed crimes and Brian was mistaken for his identical twin. Eventually the two brother's trails crossed and there was a bitter/sweet reunion before Brent had to escape a San Antonio posse.

It was during this escape that Brent happened upon a woman who had been wounded and her husband killed by cowhands of a ruthless rancher who thought they were 'squatters'. Eventually the two fell in love and were married.

Knowing it was just a matter of time before the law would catch up to him if he remained in Texas, Brent decided to head out West to California. Hoping to get a fresh start in life, Brent and his new bride Julia, along with a young man named Grant Holt and Holt's infant baby daughter, struck out by wagon on their trek westward.

Along the way they joined up with a wagon train where they met a man named Denver Dobbs, a gambler. Dobbs had met Brent in Crystal City, Texas when Brent was a deputy sheriff there. Dobbs did not recall the meeting, however.

When Dobbs accidentally ran across a 'wanted poster' on Brent he saw a way of picking up some 'easy money' that would help him get his start in California. His plan was foiled, however, when they picked up two children, Hank and Annie Thurston who had lost their adopted parents when bandits had robbed and killed them along the Southern Emigrant Trail.

The little girl, Annie, had found the wanted poster in Dobbs's wagon and used it as a make believe blanket for her rag doll. When Sackett saw the poster he confronted Dobbs with it. Dobbs swore he had never intended to try and collect on the reward money, but Brent didn't trust the man.

Meanwhile, AJ Sackett, having recovered from his gunshot wound, and his brother Brian were on the trail of two men, Rawhide Deacon and Snake Eyes Bob, who had tried to kill their father and had headed for the Mexican border. The two brothers followed the men to San Felipe del Rio where they killed the brother of Deacon, who was the sheriff of San Felipe del Rio.
    The Sackett brothers then tracked Deacon and Snake Eyes Bob across the border and into Mexico. Knowing they had to bring the men back alive in order to clear their name for killing Deacon's brother put even more pressure on the two Sackett brothers.
    Our story picks up with Brent, Julia and the others traveling along the Southern Emigrant Trail about 50 miles east of Las Cruces, New Mexico.

Raymond D. Mason

Chapter 1

BRENT SACKETT watched Denver Dobbs with a critical eye as the man carried a bucket of water from a small watering hole back to his wagon and dumped it into the water barrel mounted on the side of his wagon. Julia noticed and sensed what was going through Brent's mind. Brent had shared his feelings about Dobbs with her enough times; that was for sure.

"Do you really think Dobbs will turn you in the first chance he gets?" Julia asked quietly.

"I do. He's a gambler and he's just waiting until the odds are in his favor. I figure it will come once we get to California. He needs us right now, but once we arrive there all bets are off," Brent said with a scowl.

"I notice how he watches you when he knows you're not looking. When he sees me watching him, though, he quickly looks away," Julia stated.

"He's sizing me up. Again, he's working out all the details in that gambler's mind of his."

"Perhaps we're reading too much into the fact that he had that wanted poster on you, Brent. Maybe he just wanted to use that poster for leverage to get you to allow him to travel with us like he said," Julia whispered.

Brent shook his head negatively, "No, I don't see it that way. If he'd wanted to do that he would've just shown it to me as soon as he caught up to us. You saw how he was when he realized he'd been caught with the 'goods'. Right away he tried to shift the blame to me, saying I was the one hiding things," Brent stated.

"I just want us to get to California and start our new life. Why do these things have to happen," Julia asked looking at Brent with a downcast look in her eyes.

Brent looked at her lovingly for a moment and then put his arm around her shoulder. She looked up into his face and he smiled as he cupped her face in his hands and kissed her tenderly.

When their lips parted he said softly, "I don't want you to worry, do you hear me? Everything's going to be all right. You let me handle the worrying".

"I love you, Brent. I just want us to be happy."

"We are happy, aren't we?"

"Yes, we are. Maybe I should have said I just want us to be left alone so we can enjoy our happiness," Julia said thoughtfully.

Dobbs finished with his chores and walked over to where Brent and Julia were seated by their wagon. When he reached them he knelt down on one knee and smiled.

Julia stood up and before Dobbs could say anything said she had to check on the baby. Brent watched her as she walked away and then turned his attention towards Dobbs.

Dobbs looked at Brent with a serious look etched on his narrow face and said, "I've been doing some thinking, Sackett. Once we get to Las Cruces I'm going to go on alone. You are convinced that I'm after the reward money that's on your head and this is causing too much tension between us.

"I don't want to have to worry about closing my eyes at night for fear of not waking up in the morning. As soon as we reach Las Cruces I'll be leaving you," Dobbs said seriously.

Brent eyed him curiously for several seconds before finally replying.

"You could always turn me in to the sheriff in Las Cruces. That reward would still be honored."

"Yeah, but then we're right back to square one, ain't we. I don't need the reward money, Sackett. I've got a good stake for when I arrive in California. And, to be honest, if I was to need more money I'm good enough at cards to win it. No, the best thing for us to do is part company," Dobbs said seriously.

Brent pondered Dobbs's words and then replied, "That might be the best thing to do; but, you shouldn't lose any sleep worrying about what I might do while you're sleeping. If I was going to do anything to you, you'd know it. I'd only cut your throat if I thought I couldn't take you...and I've never met a man yet that I didn't think I could take in a gunfight."

Dobbs' eyes widened at Brent's words as Brent went on.

"Maybe we'll run into a good sized wagon train heading west. If we do, we'll both join up with them. I think we'd both feel a whole lot better then," Brent said.

"The odds of us running across others making the move are highly doubtful. I'm a gambler, remember. I like the odds of the 'house' over the odds of the player. As long as we're traveling together you hold the 'house odds'," Dobbs said and forced a slight grin.

"If I just had some guarantee you wouldn't turn me in, Dobbs, everything would be different. Julia and I just want to start over and California looked like our best bet. With this wanted poster you've cast a dark shroud over our move," Brent said evenly.

"To be honest, I wish I hadn't picked that blasted poster up now. I don't even know why I did it. I wasn't even sure it was you when I first looked at it. Just the fact that you were sportin' the same first name made me wonder if it was you. That full beard you're wearing now makes identifying you a lot more difficult," Dobbs said.

"Well, we should be in Las Cruces in another four to five days. Let me know what you're planning on doing," Brent stated as Julia walked up to where the two men were standing.

"She's sleeping like a little angel," Julia said with a smile.

Dobbs nodded and then excused himself by saying, "Well, I guess I've said all I have to say about my decision. You folks have a good night. I'll see you in the morning."

As he walked away Julia watched him for a few seconds and then looked up into Brent's eyes, "What was that all about?"

"Dobbs is leaving us once we reach Las Cruces. He said he was tired of sleeping with one eye open. It's better if we do part company, I guess," Brent said feeling as though a great weight had been lifted off his shoulders.

Julia smiled as she closed her eyes and whispered, "Thank you, Lord."

"What?" Brent questioned.

"I was just thanking the Lord for answering a prayer. I asked Him to do something to bring us to the right decision. It looks like He has honored my request," Julia said.

"You really believe that, huh?" Brent asked.

"Yes, I do," Julia said seriously.

"Well, if it was His doing I'll thank Him too," Brent smiled.

Raymond D. Mason

Chapter 2

**A Small Mexican Village
South of the Mexican Border**

BRIAN AND AJ SACKETT tied their mounts' bridle reins to a small hitching rail in front of a cantina. They had lost the trail of Rawhide Deacon and Snake Eyes Bob, but felt they could pick it up without too much trouble come sunup.

"Man, am I beat," Brian said as he stretched his back muscles.

"I know that feeling, Brian. Let's hope they've got something beside beans and tortillas in this cantina," AJ said.

The two men entered the cantina and found that there were only six other people in the whole place. The bartender spoke some English, and when he saw the two American cowboys smiled widely.

"Greetings, my friends; what is it I may get for you both?" he asked proudly.

"Tequila...a bottle," AJ said and then asked, "What do you have to eat?"

"Oh, we have frijoles and tortillas; and we have, uh, the how you say...hard huevos...the hard eggs; and the chicken and the dog meat."

Brian had already taken a table and had his long legs stretched out with his eyes closed. AJ gave his brother a quick look and shook his head.

"He could go to sleep during a cattle stampede," he said under his breath and then said quickly as he realized what the bartender had said, "Dog meat?"

When the bartender set the bottle of Tequila on the bar with two glasses, AJ said, "We'll have a chicken, and frijoles and tortillas and bring them to the table."

AJ picked up the bottle of Tequila and the two glasses and walked to the table where Brian was sitting.

"I hope you're comfortable, little brother," AJ said as he set the bottle and glasses down on the table.

"I'm in hog heaven, AJ. But, as for that 'little brother' tag you've put on me, have you noticed I'm a good two inches taller than you," Brian said with his eyes closed and a slight grin.

"You'll always be my 'little' brother. Here, tie into this Tequila. The bartender is gettin' us some vittles to eat. I hope you like chicken, beans and tortillas and hard boiled eggs. I passed on the dog meat," AJ said as he threw his leg over the back of a chair and sat down.

"Right now I'd eat the chicken raw that laid those eggs, as well as the eggs," Brian said as he opened his eyes and after a moment said, "Dog?"

Just then a young Mexican woman walked up to the table carrying a large tray with a small bowl of hard boiled eggs, two plates containing two rather small chickens, and a couple of tortillas wrapped around some refried beans.

AJ looked up at the young woman and then said to Brian, "Pay the lady, Brian. I got the Tequila and carried it over here."

Brian grinned as he dug into his pocket and dug out a five dollar gold piece. He tossed it onto the tray and the woman smiled warmly at him. AJ noticed and broke into a smile.

"What's so funny?" Brian asked when he saw his brother's grin.

"I think she wants to know how you want your change; in money or trade," AJ chuckled.

"Money...," Brian said and gave the woman a closer look. "...Maybe," he then added, getting another chuckle from AJ.

Just then four men entered the cantina. Two of the men were Mexican; one had two bandoliers crisscrossing his shoulders and chest. One of the men was a black man, and the fourth was white. They all carried the look of hard cases. Their gazes locked onto the Sackett brothers instantly as they made their way to the bar.

AJ looked at the four men and then glanced at Brian who was still eyeing the young woman. AJ kicked his brother's foot and gave a head nod in the direction of the four men.

Brian looked at the men and then back at AJ and gave a questioning frown. AJ slowly shook his head as he placed his hand on his gun, indicating the men were more than likely hired guns, or bandits.

Brian nodded his acknowledgement and then returned his gaze at the young woman who was walking back to the bar to get his change.

"It looks like some men on the run," AJ said for Brian's ears only.

"Looks that way; I wonder who they're running from?"

"Or who they're working for, might be a more appropriate question," AJ answered.

The Gringo turned around and gave the Sackett brothers a steady stare. AJ glanced up and noticed. When AJ looked away the Gringo called out to him.

"Where are you two from," the man asked?

AJ and Brian gave one another a quick look before they both looked in the man's direction.

"Who wants to know?" AJ asked.

The Gringo stood a little taller as he replied, "I do."

AJ gave the man a stone faced stare as he said, "We're right back to the first question...who are you?"

"The name's Billy Cornett, if you have to know. Now, you answer my question...where are you two from?"

AJ grinned slightly before answering, "Texas."

Cornett gave a disgusted look as he said, "Texas...now that's saying something. Texas is as big as all outdoors and you say that's where you're from. What part of Texas?"

"All of it," Brian cut in.

"You're from all of Texas? All! Why won't you just give me a simple answer? What part of 'all of Texas' are you boys from," Cornett went on?

Brian chuckled, "Up in Taylor County. Does that satisfy your curiosity?"

Cornett nodded slightly as he replied, "Now that wasn't so hard was it, girls?

AJ slowly got to his feet and turned to face Cornett and the other three men with him.

"What was that crack?" AJ said as Brian also got to his feet.

Cornett widened his stance slightly as his eyes darted from one Sackett to the next. One of the Mexican men turned and glared at Cornett.

"Hey, Billy...no trouble in here," the Mexican with the bandoliers said with a frown. "We've got more important work to do."

Cornett cast a quick look at the Mexican and then back at AJ and Brian. He slowly moved his hand away from his gun and started to turn his back on the two brothers.

"We're not finished here," AJ said firmly. "I want an apology from you for that crack you just made."

"That goes for me, too," Brian stated.

Cornett looked over his shoulder at them and then at the Mexican man with the bandoliers. His teeth clenched in anger, Cornett muttered barely audible, "I'm sorry for the slur."

"What was that?" AJ asked. "I don't think everyone in here heard that apology. Louder."

Cornett gritted his teeth again as he glared at AJ.

"I'll be damned if I will," Billy said and went for his gun.

AJ's hand moved like lightning as he drew and fired, just as Cornett's gun was moving upwards out of the holster. Billy's shot went wild as he fell back against the bar and then face forward to the floor.

Brian's draw was just as fast, but he leveled his gun at the other three men who had their hands over their pistol grips but never tried to draw them. The Mexican who had warned Billy held his hands out in front of him.

"It was his play...not ours," he said quickly.

AJ and Brian's eyes darted around the room to make sure no one else was drawing down on them. Satisfied that no one was going for their gun, the two brothers picked up their tortillas and beans and moved to the door of the cantina.

"You boys interrupted a much needed rest, but I think it would be better if we go," AJ said as he and Brian backed out of the cantina.

"Wait a minute," Brian said and hurried back to the table and grabbed the bottle of Tequila.

"I think we might need this. Besides….I paid for it," he said.

Chapter 3

20 miles east of Las Cruces

SHORTLY BEFORE dawn Brent Sackett stuck an extra pistol in the top of his boot as a 'back up' before saddling his horse. When he heard something behind him he whirled around quickly to find Hank Thurston standing there with a frown on his young face.

"You're not leaving us...are you, Mr. Johnson?"

"No, why do you ask that, Hank?"

"I heard you and Mr. Dobbs talking last night. It sounded like you were in trouble. I hope not," Hank said.

"No, it's just that Mr. Dobbs will be leaving us when we get to Las Cruces. We'll be going on alone," Brent explained.

"Good. I don't like Mr. Dobbs. He isn't nice to Annie. He's always calling her a little brat. Annie and I like you and your wife...but, not him."

"Well, he won't be with us much longer. I've got to ride out and see what's up ahead. We should be getting close to Las Cruces. I won't be gone long. You'd better go and grab yourself something to eat,"

Brent said as he tightened the cinch down and flipped the right bridle rein up over his horse's neck.

Stepping up onto his mount, Brent looked down at Hank and said, "Tell Julia I'll be back in a couple of hours. Once she's put things away tell her I said to head on up the trail."

"Okay," Hank said.

Brent reined his horse around and kicked it into an easy lope as he headed up the trail. He'd been letting Grant Holt do most of the scouting ahead and it felt good to be back in the saddle again.

About two and a half miles from where he'd left the wagons Brent topped a hill and looked down the other side. As he scoured the landscape and the trail ahead he suddenly looked off to his right. That's when his eyes locked onto ten riders below. They were heading south at a slow gallop.

Brent reached into his saddlebags and pulled out the telescope that he had picked up before they struck out for California. He zeroed in on the lead rider and the first thing he noticed was the size of the man. Brent could tell the man was well over six feet tall.

Brent put the glass on each of the other riders and found that five of the nine were wearing Mexican attire and sombreros. One of the white men was wearing a Confederate soldier's cap. One was wearing a Derby hat, and the other two were wearing Western style hats.

"They've got to be a gang of 'law benders'," Brent said to himself.

He continued to watch the men as they made their way along the valley floor. When they reached the trail the wagon trains followed they turned west towards Las Cruces.

"I hope you guys aren't planning on staying long in Las Cruces. You spell trouble," Brent said under his breath.

What Brent saw next really bothered him. As he continued to watch the men they rode to a spot just off the trail and it appeared they were making camp there.

"No...don't stay there; move on," Brent muttered. "The sun just came up, for crying out loud...don't make camp."

The Sackett Ranch

John Sackett was sitting up in bed with the doctor looking on. The doctor had just finished putting his stethoscope away and was closing up his bag.

"You Sackett's are some of the fastest healing people I've ever seen, John. Most people would only show about half the improvement you do. I should know! I've patched up enough of you," the doctor said.

"It's just part of our makeup I guess," John said. "Why, I had a great uncle who lost his arm while working on a loading dock in San Francisco and a week later he'd grown himself a new one," John said with a chuckle.

"I know you're on the mend now. Only a healthy man would make the effort to tell a bad joke like that," the doctor said with his own laugh.

John's daughter Lisa, who was in the upstairs bedroom with the two men, looked out the window. She did a double take and then turned to her father.

"Dad, someone just rode up out in front in a carriage and is tying up at the hitching rail," Lisa said.

"A carriage," John commented. "Who is it, can you tell?" he then asked.

Lisa looked out again and took a closer look this time, "It's a man and a woman...oh my Gosh," she exclaimed excitedly. "It's Uncle Dave and Tammy Jo."

"You're kidding...did you telegraph them about my being shot?" John asked quickly.

"No, I didn't. To be honest I didn't even think about it due to the seriousness of your wound. I was too busy thinking about you, I guess," Lisa said and started for the door.

"Oh, it will be so good to see them again. Tammy Jo must have a million things to tell me about finishing school," Lisa said as she rushed out the door and down the hallway to the stairs.

"Dave is your brother, isn't he, John?" the doctor asked.

"Yeah; he's from St. Louis, Missouri...I haven't seen him in over four, five years," John said as he sat a little more upright in bed.

Suddenly the smile dropped from his face and he took on a more serious look.

"If Lisa didn't wire Dave about the shooting I wonder what it is that brought him down here," John asked himself.

"You're about to find out. It sounds like Lisa is greeting them right now," the doctor said with a light laugh.

"Hey Doc, thanks a million for coming out. See Lisa and she'll settle up with you," John said extending his hand to the doctor.

The doctor shook hands with John and then walked to the door.

"I'll be back in a week or ten days. Knowing you though, you'll probably be up busting broncs by then," the doctor laughed.

"Not likely...not anymore; take care, Doc," John said.

The doctor walked out and met Lisa coming up the stairs with Dave and Tammy Jo Sackett in tow. The doctor tipped his hat as he passed them by. When they got to John's bedroom Dave peeked around the corner of the door.

"Well, well, well. So you finally found something that will force you to take it easy, huh?" Dave said with a grin.

"Yeah, a couple of .44 slugs will do it every time," John said with a wide smile. "How've you been, Dave?"

Just then Tammy Jo rounded the corner holding Lisa's hand. Tammy let go of her sister's hand and rushed to John's side.

"Oh Dad...I'm so glad you're okay. How bad was your wound? Who did this to you? Where are Brian and AJ; why aren't they here?" Tammy asked a flurry of questions.

"Whoa, whoa," John said laughingly, "one question at a time, little girl."

"I'll answer the last question for Tammy, Dad," Lisa said and when she got the go ahead nod from her father proceeded with her statement.

"AJ and Brian went after the men who tried to kill, Dad. They'll get them too, and then they'll come back to the ranch," Lisa said, sounding more hopeful than forceful.

Tammy looked sad for a moment and tears filled her eyes. Lisa noticed and put her hand on her sister's shoulder.

"What is it, Tam?" she asked softly and in a very caring tone of voice.

"I wish Brent was here. There's still no word from him?" she asked.

"Oh, yes there is. Brian and AJ found out he was living up in Lubbock County and went up and met him and his wife," Lisa said with a smile.

"His wife?" Tammy Jo exclaimed. "You mean he's married now?"

"Yes, and according to Brian and AJ she is really a sweet girl and very pretty."

"Is he coming back here to the ranch? Did he say?" Tammy asked.

Lisa shook her head slowly and said, "No, they are on their way to California." She then looked to make sure no one else was listening and whispered, "Brent's in a little trouble; that's the reason for moving out to California."

"Well, if he lets us know where they settle down I just may take a trip out there to see them," Tammy replied.

"Hey, I'll go with you. I'd love to see Brent and meet his wife. And, I've always wanted to see what California was like," Lisa said excitedly.

"Oh, wouldn't that be a fun trip?" Tammy said and hugged her sister.

"Hey, hey," John said feigning seriousness, "...I don't know that California is ready for you two out there yet. They may never be the same."

The girls laughed as they looked at one another and then touched John's face lovingly.

Chapter

4

DENVER DOBBS wore a deep frown as he followed the Sackett's wagon in his own wagon along the narrow trail. He'd hoped to collect on the reward posted for Brent, but now he'd have to work things out a little differently.

Dobbs plan had been to make sure Brent was alive when they reached Las Cruces and turn him in to the local authorities there. Now it would be more difficult. He felt he would have to kill Sackett in order to collect the reward. The thing that bothered him now though, was what he would do about Julia, the Thurston kids, and Grant Holt and his baby.

Dobbs knew that Brent wouldn't be easy to bring down. He also knew he would have to be very careful in setting up his plan. If Sackett got wind of what he planned the whole idea could blow up in his face. The timing would have to be just right. But first he'd have to figure out what to do about Julia and the others.

In the meantime Brent had been keeping a watchful eye on the ten horsemen he'd spotted. It appeared they were making camp alongside a small stream. The campsite they'd chosen was only about forty yards off the wagon trail. And that was much too close for Brent's liking.

Riding to a point where he could not be seen by the ten men, Brent looked for a way around the camp. It became quite obvious that the men had deliberately picked that spot because there was no passable route for wagons to get around them.

Brent quickly made up his mind. He kicked his horse into a gallop and headed back towards the wagons. He'd have them make camp wherever they could find a secluded spot away from the trail. They'd have to wait the men out. Hopefully the men would move on at sun-up the next day. If the gang didn't move on, then Brent and the others would be forced to simply wait until they did so.

This didn't set well with Brent. If it was just himself he had to worry about it would be a lot simpler. He'd wait until dark and try to get by the gang. If they saw him and tried anything he'd take his chances. Shoot it out with them and then hightail it out of there.

The sudden movement to Brent's right broke into his thoughts. Something was moving through a small grove of trees. He didn't have any idea what it might be; man or beast, but something definitely was moving around amongst the trees.

As he galloped along keeping a wary eye on the tree line he didn't see the rope that had been tied across the trail. His horse passed under the rope, but Brent didn't. One second he was in the saddle and the next he was laying on the ground with the wind knocked out of him.

Brent lay there for a moment stunned by what had happened. Just as the realization hit him as to what had happened two men on horseback rode up and looked down at him. They both had their pistols drawn and aimed at him.

"Well, well, look what we have here, Navarro. What do you think a man would be doing riding all alone out here in the middle of nowhere?" the white man said with a twisted grin.

"I don't know. What do you think he is doing out here, Amigo?"

"I think he's about to get robbed. This is dangerous country around here," the white man said with a grin.

"Do you have any money on you, hombre?" the man named Navarro asked.

Brent, still somewhat shaken by the fall, muttered, "Why don't you get down and check?"

The white man bristled and cocked the hammer back on his pistol as he snarled, "You're in no position to get smart, hoss. Now give us what money you have before I blow your head off."

"It's in my boot," Brent said as he slowly got to his feet.

"Well...get it," the Gringo snapped angrily.

Brent slowly bent over and reached down in the top of his boot. With lightning speed Brent moved to his right while bringing the pistol up that he had put in his boot top earlier. His quickness took both men by surprise.

The first shot hit the white man in the chest; the second shot hit the Mexican in the throat. Both men fell from their saddles and hit the ground hard. The Mexican died quickly, but the Gringo lingered long enough for Brent to ask him a few questions.

Hurrying over to where the wounded man was, Brent bent over him and asked, "Who are you? Are you with the men camped down in the valley?"

Laboring to get a breath the white man replied, "I'm dying; man you've killed me."

"You were about to kill me. Now tell me, are you with the men camped in the valley?" Brent asked again.

"Yeah, Lomax...Sam Lomax; it's his gang. Don't let me die like this. Pray for me. I don't want to go hell," the man said wide eyed.

"You pray. You're the one dying, not me. Just say the 'sinner's prayer'," Brent said sternly.

"I ain't prayed before; not that I can remember, anyway. What do I say?"

"You want to be forgiven, don't you? Ask the Lord to forgive you I guess. Who is this Sam Lomax?"

The man didn't answer Brent's question. He was too busy attempting to make peace with God. It wasn't the usual sinner's prayer; that was for sure.

"Lord, I've been a skunk most of my life. I've cheated, and drank, chewed, had women, stole things, shot people, and lied every time I needed to get out of a jam. I didn't like very many people and even fewer liked me. I don't want to go to hell, though Lord. Will you let me in through those gates of pearl? I promise I'll be...," he said just before he died.

Brent looked down at him and shook his head as he said, "Live like the devil and then ask to be a saint. Good luck whoever you are because you're going to need it."

Brent went through the dead men's pockets and relieved them of what money they had been carrying. He found several gold rings and lockets with small photos in them, obviously possessions they had stolen from people they had robbed. After counting the money he had lifted off the men he picked up their pistols and shoved them under his belt.

When Brent had passed under the rope and been knocked to the ground, his horse had run on down the trail about a hundred yards before stopping to graze. The bandit's horses had merely moved a couple dozen yards away.

Brent moved slowly up to one of the bandit's horse and caught the bridle reins. He loaded the guns he'd taken off the men into the saddlebags and after giving the two dead men's bodies another quick look mounted up taking the reins of the other man's horse as well and riding down the trail towards his horse.

When Brent reached his mount he rode up to it and grabbed the reins and wrapped them around the saddle horn on the horse he was riding. There was no sense in leaving the horses to roam free. Besides, he didn't want them wandering down to the valley floor to where the gang was camped and tipping them off that they'd lost a couple members of their gang.

Meanwhile, back at the wagons, Dobbs had stopped what he was doing and listened intently. He thought he'd heard the sound of gunfire, but couldn't be sure. The shots sounded far off, but he wasn't exactly sure if what he'd heard was gunshots or not. Julia noticed his intensity and asked him about it.

"Are you all right Mr. Dobbs?"

"Yes, I'm fine...Did you hear what sounded like gunshots just now?" he asked.

"I heard something off in the distance...I guess it could have been gunshots," Julia replied.

Dobbs instantly feared that something might have happened to Brent, thus spoiling his plan of cashing in on the reward money that was on Sackett's head.

"I take it your husband has not returned yet; am I right?"

"That's right...he left early this morning. He wanted to check out the trail ahead and said he would be back once he had."

"Did he say anything else?" Dobbs asked with a frown.

"No, he didn't. Do you think the gunshots could have been Brent's?" Julia asked concernedly.

Dobbs nodded yes and then said, "Yeah, or shots taken at him."

Julia cringed at Dobbs's words. He noticed and quickly added, "He's all right; you can be sure of that."

"Maybe we should go and see what happened?" Julia wondered aloud.

"I think we should get going. He could have run across Indians...or bandits. These mountains are full of gangs of bandits," Dobbs said as he had the germ of an idea form in his mind.

Dobbs figured this could be the opportunity he was looking for; a dead Brent Sackett and he wouldn't even have to do the killing. He'd just haul the body on into Las Cruces and claim the reward there. That would also solve his dilemma about Julia and the others.

Dobbs couldn't hold back a smile; something that Julia caught, but didn't comment on. Now she truly didn't trust the man. If he was conjuring up something she wanted to know what it was, but how would she find out; that was the question?

Dobbs saw Brent and felt his heart drop. He knew now he'd have to do his own killing. He'd wait until the right opportunity and when it presented itself he'd do what he had to do.

Dobbs jumped down off his wagon and ran up alongside the Sackett's wagon when he saw Brent approaching riding the bandit's horse and leading two others.

"Where'd you get the horses?" Dobbs called out when Brent rode up.

"Off two men who tried to rob me," Brent said, and then added. "I'll tell you all about it later. Right now we've got to find a good campsite off the trail that's well hidden. We've got a few people in the area that I don't want knowing we're here."

"Do you mean bandits?" Dobbs asked.

"Yep, bandits...have you ever heard of a man by the name of Sam Lomax?" Brent asked Dobbs.

"Lomax, Lomax...yeah, I've heard tell of him. Is it his gang that's around here?" Dobbs asked.

"Yeah, that's what one of the men I shot said just before he died," Brent replied.

Dobbs' eyes widened slightly at Brent's words as Sackett went to the saddlebags of the horse that Slater had been riding. When he opened the flap he looked quickly at Dobbs who was looking down at the ground obviously in thought.

Brent didn't let on that he'd just found six sticks of dynamite in the bags. He quickly pulled the saddlebags off the horse and carried them to his wagon. This dynamite may be just what the doctor ordered to get them by the outlaw gang.

Dobbs was still deep in thought and never paid that much attention to what Brent did with the saddlebags and didn't even know what Brent had found in them.

This man wasn't going to go down easy, Dobbs thought to himself. One mistake on his part and it could be his last. Maybe he'd have to wait until they got to Las Cruces after all. Let a lawman put his life on the line.

Chapter

5

BRIAN AND AJ reined their horses to a halt when they reached the top of a rise that would give them a good view of the landscape ahead. Brian started to turn and say something to AJ when something off to his left caught his eye. He turned his full attention towards it and realized it was a man lying on the ground about two hundred yards away.

"Over there, AJ," Brian said and reined his horse in the man's direction.

AJ followed along behind as they both kicked their horses into a gallop. When they reached the spot where the man lay, Brian stepped down off his horse while AJ scoured the surrounding area in case this was an ambush.

The man was a Mexican man in his late fifties; he was alive, but just barely. He'd been shot in the side and had lost a lot of blood. Brian immediately attempted to stop the bleeding. When he turned the man on his side, Brian could see that the bullet had passed cleanly through.

Once AJ was assured this was not an ambush he climbed down off his horse and grabbed his canteen. Moving up alongside Brian, AJ poured a little bit of water onto the man's lips.

When the water worked its magic on the man he opened his eyes. When he did, AJ gave him a little more water to drink. The man blinked several times and tried to speak.

"Two men..." he said in broken English and in a mere whisper.

Brian looked quickly at AJ and then back at the man and asked, "Were they Gringos?"

The man blinked his eyes and muttered, "Si."

Brian continued to work over the man and finally managed to stop the bleeding somewhat. AJ kept giving the man sips of water and after about fifteen minutes the man seemed to be a little stronger.

"Where are you from?" Brian asked the man.

"My farm is just over that hill," the man said in his broken English.

"We'll get you home, Amigo," Brian said and looked up at AJ.

AJ was gazing in the direction of the next ridge and figured it to be about three miles away. Together Brian and AJ got the old man on his feet and onto Brian's horse.

With the old Mexican man in the saddle and slumped out over the horse's neck Brian climbed on in back of him and they headed in the direction of the man's farm. Fortunately the short ride didn't injure the man anymore than he already was, but when they arrived at his farm they had another surprise.

The old Mexican's wife had been pistol whipped and was lying unconscious on the floor of the small house. AJ attended to her while Brian carried the old man inside the house and laid him on the only bed they had.

"Looks like more handiwork of Rawhide and Snake Eyes," AJ said.

Looking around the small house Brian shook his head negatively, "What could they possibly have found in here to steal?"

"Food, more than likely," AJ replied.

"I'll be so glad when we catch up to these two. I don't know if they're worth taking back alive," Brian snapped angrily.

"I know how you feel, but remember. They may keep us from being hung from the nearest tree. I'm sure there are wanted posters out on them. I've had my suspicions about those two ever since they went to work for us.

"Remember how they used to take off for a couple days at a time on some excuse and then we'd hear a couple of weeks later about a stagecoach holdup, or cattle missing from one of the other ranches. I think they were the ones responsible. I didn't at the time, but now I do," AJ said evenly.

"I know one thing for sure," Brian said as he gave AJ a quick glance, "Neither one of them could play cards without cheating. I thought the boys were going to kill 'em a couple of times. They probably would have if I hadn't stopped them in time."

"What did you stop them for," AJ said with a wry grin?

"Just too tender hearted, I suppose," Brian said getting a chuckle from AJ.

The woman began to come around and when she saw the two Gringos standing over her put her hand to her mouth with fear showing in her eyes.

"It's all right, Ma'am," AJ said with a kind smile. "We're not going to hurt you."

Brian watched her closely and then said, "I don't think she understands English."

"Comprende English…Americano?" AJ asked her.

"No…no comprende," the woman said and then looked over to see her husband lying on the bed.

"Carlos," she said and tried to get to her feet.

"He's been shot…uh, pistol-a," Brian said.

The woman's eyes darted from one man to the other and then back to her husband. Slowly she attempted to get up, this time being helped by AJ and moved up alongside her husband.

The woman's husband began to explain to her in Spanish what had happened and that the two 'Americanos' had brought him home. They were not like the ones who had done this to them. She gave her description of the two men who'd beaten her to her husband and he passed it along to Brian and AJ. It matched the description of Rawhide and Snake Eyes.

Once Brian and AJ had made the couple comfortable and were sure they'd be all right, they mounted up and easily picked up Deacon and Snake Eyes' trail.

Brian kept an eye on the ground and the hoof prints while AJ scoured the country side for any sign of the two. It didn't take long before Brian picked up some other hoof prints as well as the ones of the two they were following.

"Looks like there're some others following our boys," Brian observed.

"Oh…how many?" AJ asked.

"I'd say eight, maybe nine riders. They can't be more than a couple of hours ahead of us; and I mean all of them," Brian said casting a quick glance at AJ.

"It could be a Mexican gang," AJ commented and then paused before he said, "or maybe Federalies."

"Let's hope it is Federalies. I don't want to tangle with a Mexican gang; not down here, anyway," Brian replied.

"Hey, we may not be any better off if it is the Federalies. You've heard some of the tales about them," AJ said.

"Yeah, most of the gangs are hated by the locals; but then so are the federal troops. Makes you wonder doesn't it," Brian said with a chuckle.

They rode another hour, still following the tracks of both groups ahead of them. When they reached a high plateau where they could see a good distance ahead, they reined up.

"Down there," AJ said as he pointed in a small valley.

It was the eight riders that had been following Deacon and Bob. It wasn't federal troopers; that was easy to see by the size of the sombreros the men were wearing.

"Deacon and Bob might be in for a little surprise," AJ said with a grin.

"Yeah, but that won't do us a whole lot of good, will it!" Brian said seriously.

"Oh, no I guess it won't. I'd hate to think we have to help them out of a tight spot over this," AJ said flashing a deep frown.

Brian continued to scour the area ahead and suddenly pointed at a spot a considerable distance ahead of the bandits.

"There they are, AJ, just topping that hill," Brian said.

"They don't know they're being followed, you can tell by the way they're riding. You'd think they were merely out on a pleasure ride," AJ observed.

"Their pleasure is going to come to a halt in about ten or fifteen minutes. We'd better try and get to them before it's too late," Brian said and the two kicked their horses into a fast gallop.

They rode down off the hill and off to the right of the path the gang had taken. Hopefully they could catch up to Deacon and Bob and get the drop on them before making a run for it from the gang.

As Brian rode along he kept having thoughts of Brent creep into his mind. Twins often sense things about one another even though they may be hundreds of miles apart. Brian felt that Brent might be in trouble wherever he was at that particular moment.

What Brian had no way of knowing, however, was at that very moment Brent was dealing with a gang of bandits, also. And it just so happened that Brent had the same identical thoughts running through his mind about Brian.

Chapter
6

SAM LOMAX took a sip of his coffee and spit it out as he bellowed, "Who made this pot of mud, anyway?"

"The Breed," Billy Boles said with a giggle.

Lomax looked at the half breed Apache and snapped, "It had to be your mama who was the Apache. No white man would make this stuff and call it coffee."

"If you don't like it, don't drink it. That's the way I like it," Chino Parker said.

"Then you just fix your own coffee from now on and let someone else fix ours," Lomax went on.

"Hey, Sam, when are we going to go on into Las Cruces, anyway? I'd like to spend some of this money we have," one of the gang members known only as Reno said.

"We'll be there tomorrow night if we leave at first light in the morning. These horses have pretty well had it and need a rest. We'll leave early tomorrow," Lomax said as he poured the remains of his coffee out of the cup.

"Here, Sam, try this," Boles said and handed Lomax a flask of whiskey.

"Where'd you get this?" Lomax asked as he took the flask from Boles.

"Off one of those nester's wagons," Boles grinned. "He had good taste in whiskey, wouldn't you say?"

Lomax took a swig of whiskey and handed the flask back to Boles, "Yeah, not bad. But then when you've been without whiskey for a week or more, anything tastes good to you."

"When are Navarro and Slater supposed to join us," Boles asked?

"I'd say any time now. I halfway expected them to be here by now, but they may have had to lose a posse before heading this way. What do you think of Navarro, anyway?" Lomax asked.

"I guess he's all right. I wouldn't want to turn my back on him if I'd crossed him though. Slater's the same way. He'd shoot you in the back in minute. I swear that man has mush for brains," Boles stated.

"Not like us, huh?" Lomax said with a half grin.

"Nothing like us," Boles replied.

"When we get to Las Cruces we'll go in teamed up. You can go with me and the others can team up and enter town in twos or threes. Everyone will go to different saloons and wait for Boles and me to show up with their orders. I don't want to be too obvious with our arrival in town. I'll fill everyone in on this tonight, or as soon as Navarro and Slater get here," Lomax said.

"How much do you think that bank has in it?" Boles asked.

"From what I was told it may have as much as eighty, ninety thousand dollars in it. It'll be a good day's haul, I can tell you that. We need Slater here though. He's the explosives man," Lomax said.

"Do you really think we'll need dynamite?" Boles questioned.

"Yeah, for two reasons that I'll tell you about later. I'll be glad when those two yahoos get here," Lomax said.

Suddenly two of the members of the gang who had been playing cards locked up in a fight. Fists began flying and one of the men fell to the ground. Lomax glared at the two combatants as he got to his feet and walked to where they were rolling on the ground.

Lomax kicked the man who was on top of the other one in the ribs, knocking him off the man and causing him to cry out in pain. When the man who had been on the ground started to get up, Lomax kicked him in the head; knocking the man unconscious.

"You busted my ribs, Lomax," the man who had been kicked first groaned.

"You're lucky I didn't kill you, Soto...both of you. I told you that whatever you do after this job in Las Cruces was your business, but until then no fighting. You two pull this stuff every time you get in a card game. After the bank job you can kill each other if you want to, but until then you'll do as I say," Lomax snapped, his forehead furrowed in a deep frown.

Holding his ribs, the downed man said, "Blade is going to get you for this."

"Blade will die trying," Lomax snapped.

"Hey Sam...here comes Foley with some camp meat," Boles said pointing off in the distance.

Lomax looked in the direction Boles was pointing and grinned, "We'll have fresh meat tonight, men. I thought those gunshots that echoed down the canyon might be those of Foley. Looks like a good sized buck."

The men all got to their feet to meet Foley and help him with the deer he had killed. They'd been living on canned goods for three days, but they'd have venison for lunch and supper.

Somewhere in Mexico

Brian and AJ rode in low spots as much as they could; avoiding the crests of hills so as not to be seen by the Mexican bandits. They were able to overtake the gang and eventually got ahead of them and gained ground on Deacon and Snake Eyes Bob.

The dry river bed the Sackett brothers had been following made a sharp bend, cutting back in the direction of Deacon and Bob. When they rounded the bend they found themselves no more than fifty yards from the two men they'd been trailing.

Deacon went for his gun the moment he realized it was Brian and AJ. It took Snake Eyes Bob a little longer for it to sink in since he had been swilling Tequila he'd taken from the Mexican couple's home.

Both Brian and AJ drew their guns and just as Deacon fired both of them did also knocking him out of the saddle and to the ground. Snake Eyes Bob then, realizing who the two men were they'd met, went for his gun, but when he saw that he stood no chance dropped it and raised his hands.

"Don't shoot, don't shoot," he yelled out.

"Come on Bob, you're going with us; and don't try and get away," AJ yelled.

"Okay, okay," Bob said and rode to where the two brothers were.

"You two had a gang of Mexican bandits following you," AJ explained, and then snapped, "Come on, let's ride."

The three of them headed back in the direction they'd come, staying in the riverbed. The gunshots had alerted the bandits to the fact that someone was nearby and off to their right. The leader of the gang, a man by the name of Pedro Montijo, ordered several of his men to go and check out the gunshots.

Montijo and his men had not been intentionally following Deacon and Bob, but merely headed in the same direction. The gunshots, however, had shone a new light on the situation.

Because Brian and AJ had managed to get ahead of the gang, the two riders topped the riverbank no more than forty yards from the Sacketts and Bob. When they saw the three of them riding hard along the river bottom they pulled their pistols and opened fire.

AJ and Brian pulled leather and began to fire back in the direction of the two bandits. Kicking their horses into full runs, the three of them rode up out of the river bank on the opposite side of where the bandits were.

The bandits weren't too keen on giving chase. They reined their horses around and headed back to report to Montijo. When they told him about the three men he asked if the men were Gringos.

"Si, Pedro...tres Gringos. They headed in the direction of the border," the men stated.

"Let them go. We have to get to Piedras Negras. What we have to do there is more important than chasing three Gringos," Montijo said.

Raymond D. Mason

Chapter 7

BRENT SACKETT looked out the back of their covered wagon just as Denver Dobbs climbed aboard one of the bandit's horses and started to ride out of camp. Julia glanced up at Brent and saw the questioning look on his face.

"What is it, Brent?" she asked.

"Dobbs...I wonder where he's going. He just rode off on one of the bandit's horses. Man I tell you, I just don't trust that guy," Brent said shaking his head negatively.

"I wish he would just ride off and never come back," Julia said as she put her hand on Brent's arm.

"That's not likely," Brent replied.

"Maybe he is going hunting to see if he can get some fresh meat for us all," Julia said thoughtfully.

"That could be. The Mexican fella's rifle is in the saddle holster. And Dobbs was saying last night how much he likes venison. That could be it."

"I hope there's none of the gang near enough to hear the gunshot if he should shoot a deer," Julia went on.

"No, he was headed back the other way from where they have made camp. We're far enough away that they couldn't hear a gunshot. I guess we will, though if he gets a deer. Listen for it and tell me if you hear it and I don't," Brent said.

Grant Holt had been asleep under the Sackett's wagon and when he heard their voices woke up. He stood up and looked in the back of the wagon with a smile on his face.

"I know where he's going," Grant said.

"You do...where?" Brent asked quickly.

"He said he wanted to ride to the top of the peak off to the right and see if he could see Las Cruces," Grant stated.

"When did he tell you that?" Brent asked.

"Last night...after we ate supper," Grant answered.

"He should have asked me about it. I could have saved him a trip. You can't see Las Cruces from up there because of the higher mountain between us and town. Oh, well, the ride might do him some good," Brent said with a grin.

"How's my little girl doing?" Grant said looking in at the sleeping baby.

"She's doing just fine," Julia said giving the baby a quick look.

"She reminds me so much of Grace," Grant said as a look of sadness swept over his face.

"She does, doesn't she," Julia stated and flashed a quick look at Brent.

"Look at these two," Brent said as he nodded towards the Thurston kids. "They're sleeping like a couple of babies themselves."

"They really are good kids, you know, Brent. Hank told me he is so happy that we are the ones who found them. He really looks up to you. He told me the other day that he wants to be just like you when he grows up," Grant said with a grin.

Brent looked quickly from Grant to Julia and his expression became serious.

"He should set his sights higher," Brent said quietly, as he thought of his past and what his future might be.

"He could do a lot worse," Julia said cocking her head to one side and giving Brent a warm smile.

Meanwhile Denver Dobbs had changed course and was riding in the direction of Las Cruces. He wanted to get a look at the campsite of Sam Lomax and his gang.

When he reached the spot that looked down on the valley floor and could see the camp he reined the horse he was riding to a halt. He just sat there on the horse for several minutes watching the camp below.

Dobbs was unaware that at that very moment someone in the camp had noticed him and called it to Lomax's attention.

"Hey, Sam, we have someone on horseback that has taken a keen interest in us. Look up on that peak behind us. Isn't that a man on horseback or are my eyes playing tricks on me," Chino Parker said.

Lomax looked towards the peak, but couldn't see anyone. He cast a quick look back at Parker and said, "You sure do have the Indian eyes. I don't see anything up there."

"Put your glass on that peak," Parker responded.

Lomax opened the flap on his saddlebag and pulled out his telescope. He held it up to his eye and adjusted it for clarity.

"You're right, Chino. We have us a curious on looker. You don't suppose he's that Texas Ranger that's been dogging us for two weeks do you," Lomax said.

"Do you want me to find out?" Chino asked.

"Yeah, yeah I do. Do you think you can get up there without him seeing you?" Lomax questioned.

Chino nodded his head yes and walked away. He walked towards a thicket that would block the view of whoever it was on the ridge. From the thicket he was able to move behind a rocky ledge and take a round about way to the top of the high peak without fear of being seen.

Dobbs sat astraddle the horse counting the number of men in the camp and surveying the surroundings. He had seen Chino Parker leave the camp area, but was unable to see where the man went when he went behind the thicket. It never occurred to him that he might be coming up behind him until it was too late.

Chino moved quietly over the hard adobe ground. When he got within twenty yards of Dobbs he stopped and looked all around to make sure there was no one else around. Satisfied there wasn't, Chino moved up closer to Dobbs without making a sound.

"Hold it right there. Don't make a move," Chino said when he was no more than six feet from where Dobbs was on his horse.

Chino's words scared Dobbs so much he almost fell out of the saddle. He snapped his head around and stared in Chino's direction. Dobbs froze when he saw the .44 aimed at him.

"Wha...who...," Dobbs sputtered.

"Just hold it right there if you don't want to spring a leak," Chino said tightly. "Step down off that horse and we'll go down to the camp so you can get a real good look," Chino said as he motioned for Dobbs to step down.

"I was just wondering who was camped down there, that's all," Dobbs said, fear showing in his eyes.

"Never mind that, get down off your horse...," Chino started to say, but suddenly stopped as he recognized the horse as having belonged to Navarro Salazar.

"Where'd you get this horse," Chino snapped angrily?

"I found it...it came trotting down the trail," Dobbs said, quickly coming up with a lie. "That's what I'm doing here. I wanted to see if I could find the horse's owner."

"I'll bet that's what you're doing here. Come on, get off there or I'll shoot you right now," Chino growled.

Dobbs quickly got off the horse and Chino climbed aboard. He motioned with the pistol for Dobbs to start the trek down the mountainside. The two of them headed out with Chino riding along behind the walking Dobbs.

"So you were just bringing the horse back to its rightful owner, huh?" Lomax said with a frown. "Now why is it I find that hard to believe? Would you tell me that?"

"Look, there're a number of us up on the mountain there traveling by wagon and this horse came trotting down the trail where we'd made camp. I said I was going to find out where the horse came from and headed in this direction. That's all there is to it," Dobbs said with a nervous grin.

"How many of you are there?" Lomax questioned.

"Ten...fifteen," Dobbs stammered.

"Well, which is it; ten or fifteen? Don't tell me you don't know how many are traveling with you," Lomax snapped angrily.

One of the gang members named Montana had been studying Dobbs' face feeling he'd seen him before. Montana just couldn't remember where it was at first. Suddenly he recalled.

"Hey, I know this bird," Montana said.

Lomax looked quickly from Dobbs to Montana and then back at Dobbs.

"Oh, yeah...where do you know him from?"

"Dallas, when we were there. We played poker together," Montana recalled correctly.

"Is that right, hoss? Were you playing cards with Montana back in Dallas?" Lomax questioned.

"It could be. I travel a lot," Dobbs said.

"I'll bet you do," Lomax replied, "and probably one jump ahead of the law. What is your name?"

Dobbs looked quickly at the man called Montana and then said, "Dobbs...Denver Dobbs."

"Oh, it's Denver Dobbs, huh?" Lomax said and then added, "That sounds about as true as someone calling himself Montana."

The others in the gang laughed at Lomax's remark. The looks coming from all the men said they didn't believe a word Dobbs was saying.

"Let's use him for target practice for throwing our knives," one of the men said.

"Yeah...I say he shot Navarro and Slater both. They were coming to join us together, weren't they Sam?" one of the other gang members asked.

"Yeah, that's what I figured. But, where's Slater's horse? We can afford to lose Navarro, but we need Slater," Lomax said tight lipped.

"What did you do with Slater's horse?" Montana asked sharply?

"I told you what happened, honest," Dobbs said pleadingly.

Dobbs knew he was in trouble. If he could only shift the blame to someone else he might be able to save his own hide. He began to come up with a plausible explanation for what had happened. If only the gang would accept it.

What Dobbs didn't know was that there was an undercover Texas Ranger who had been accepted into the gang named Manny Chavez. He was hoping to get word to the sheriff in Las Cruces that the gang was planning to rob the bank there.

Lomax had committed a number of robberies throughout Texas and the Texas Rangers had been after him for over four years. Chavez had finally caught up with Lomax, but had to pretend to be one of the gang in order to bring about his capture.

Chavez had been responsible for capturing a number of desperados during his six year service with the Rangers. He was one of the best trackers the Rangers had working for them and had been said to be able to track a water moccasin across water.

Now, he had to see about freeing this man named Dobbs. There was another person that Chavez would have to get free from the gang as well; a woman. The bandits had taken her captive when they attacked one of the wagons along the trail. They had her dressed in men's clothing and forced her to wear a Mexican sombrero.

Dobbs had noticed one of the 'men' sitting between two other men and keeping 'his' head down as though avoiding his gaze. It wasn't until he glanced at her the third time that he realized it wasn't a man after all, but a woman. He didn't let on that he had picked up on it, though, knowing it would be best to keep his mouth shut.

Chapter
8

BRENT PEERED down on the outlaw camp from atop the same high peek from where Dobbs had been watching when he was spotted. The difference was that Brent stayed low and well hidden.

He had followed the tracks of the horse Dobbs had been riding to this very spot, and knew that Dobbs had more than likely been captured. He thought he could make out Dobbs in the camp below, but wasn't one hundred percent sure it was him.

"That idiot," Brent said softly. "Why couldn't he leave well enough alone?"

Brent looked around the area near the camp and the best way for a man to get down close to it without being seen. He realized he could go back about twenty five yards and move undetected all the way down the mountainside to a thicket not more than fifteen yards from the camp. It was the same route that Chino had taken up to where he captured Dobbs.

As much as he was tempted to just leave Dobbs there, something told him he should try and help him escape. He didn't know it at the time, but he would have help in doing just that. An undercover Texas Ranger by the name of Manny Chavez!

Brent stayed low as he backed out of sight from the camp below. He led his horse to a spot where it could graze and tethered it to a fallen tree limb. Then he began his descent down the mountainside. He noticed the tracks Chino had made when he climbed the mountain.

Once Brent had reached a spot where he could tell what the terrain was like the rest of the way down to the thicket, he turned and climbed back up the mountain. He would wait until just before dark and then go all the way down to the camp. First, however, he wanted to let Julia know what he was up too.

"Do you have to go down there, Brent? What if they catch you? I wish you'd reconsider and stay here with us. Dobbs got himself into this, let him get himself out of it," Julia said and then slowly shook her head.

"No, that wouldn't be right, I know. Still, it would solve one of our problems…wouldn't it?" she asked.

"I'm not sure it would. He might tell them about us. If he did there'd be a passel of 'em up here shortly afterwards," Brent said seriously.

"You'll be careful?" Julia said with a pleading in her eyes as well as in her voice.

"Yes, I'll be careful…I promise. I have a plan, that, if it works…could get the gang completely out of the way so we can pass," Brent said seriously and then looked at Grant.

"Grant I want you to drive Dobbs wagon to where I show you to stop and wait. Julia, I want you to follow Grant in our wagon. I'll explain what I want each of you to do once I get you in place.

"Like I said, if this little surprise I have worked out, works, you'll have to be ready and drive the horses as fast as you can through the area where the gang is camped," Brent said.

Grant nodded his head and replied, "You just tell us what to do and we'll do it; won't we Julia?"

Julia smiled at Grant and nodded her head in reply, "Yes we will."

Manny Chavez moved over by the woman the gang had taken captive and sat down. The man who had been guarding her gave Manny a quizzical look.

"I'll spell you," Manny said off handedly.

"Good, I want some coffee and some more of that stew," the man said as he got up and moved away.

Manny waited until he was out of earshot and then whispered to the woman, "Mrs. Keeling, I want you to know you have a friend in this camp."

The woman, Cheryl Keeling, looked at Chavez curiously, but didn't speak. Chavez knew he was taking a chance, but he couldn't stand idly by and allow any harm to come to an innocent bystander.

He looked around to make sure no one else was within earshot before going on.

"If anything happens you look to me for help. I am going to try and arrange a way for you to escape, but everything has to be just right. Do you hear me?" Chavez whispered firmly.

Mrs. Keeling eyed him suspiciously for a moment, but then said, "Yes, I hear you."

"I'm going to try to set it up so you and the man they captured today can both escape. I can't say when for sure, but it will be soon. I'm afraid of what the gang might do when we break camp here. You watch me and just do as I say. It might only be a motion, but you do it," Chavez went on.

"Why would you risk your life for us?" Mrs. Keeling asked.

"Never mind that now. Let it be enough to know that I am not one of the regular members of the gang. More than that I cannot say," Chavez said and then tensed slightly when he saw one of the gang headed their way.

He got to his feet quickly and glared down at Mrs. Keeling as he snapped angrily, "What do you mean by that? I'm just as good as you any day, you Gringo witch."

Mrs. Keeling was taken aback for a moment but then noticed the man approaching them.

"How dare you talk to me that way," Mrs. Keeling snapped angrily, going along with the charade.

Montana laughed as he drew near to them and called out, "What's the matter Chavez, did you get a hold of a wildcat?"

"I make one little suggestion and she gets uppity with me," Chavez said with a frown.

"I'm not used to being talked to like he just did," Mrs. Keeling said.

"Well, maybe if you'd be a little more cooperative, he wouldn't get mad at you," Montana laughed and then added. "But, you heard what Lomax said about her. Leave her alone or she won't bring a good price from Barksdale."

"Yeah, yeah, I remember," Chavez said and then asked, playing dumb, "By the way. Who is this Barksdale, anyway?"

"He runs a string of girls up to the mining camps. You know, to 'entertain' the miners. Barksdale makes more than the ones bustin' their humps looking for gold, silver, or whatever else they might be digging for, I can tell you that," Montana explained.

"I thought you knew about him?" Montana then asked curiously.

"No, I heard the name, but I didn't know what the man did. It sounds like a good business, though," Chavez grinned.

"Yeah, lettin' the ladies do all the work and he just sits back on his duff and collects the money," Montana replied.

Chavez turned his gaze towards Mrs. Keeling, "See how uppity you are when you're sold to him, woman."

"I'll die first," she answered.

On the other side of the camp Dobbs was working hard on a scheme to get out of the jam he now found himself in. He hated the idea of losing the reward money on Brent Sackett's head, but maybe that was the only way out of this.

Dobbs had been tied to a small tree at Lomax's orders and knew that he was the only one to deal with in this matter. First, though, he had to get Lomax's interest and that might not be that easy to do.

Dobbs watched Lomax closely, trying to get a fix on just what kind of man he was dealing with here. Lomax was obviously the confident type. He wasn't the kind of man who liked to follow. No, Lomax was definitely the leader type. And, he figured Lomax to be a man who liked to lead by force and by fear when he could.

Lomax glanced over towards Dobbs, but looked away. Shortly he gave his new captive another glance and saw that Dobbs was still watching him.

"Do you see something interesting?" Lomax snapped.

"I was just wondering if I should tell you about the fifteen hundred dollars I was traveling with," Dobbs said evenly.

"What is this about fifteen hundred dollars?" Lomax questioned. "You mean to tell me that you have fifteen hundred dollars on you?"

"Not on me; I said that I'm traveling with. There's a difference," Dobbs replied.

"Why don't you explain yourself a little bit better? Do you have fifteen hundred dollars with you or not?"

"I am, or should I say, was...traveling with a man who has a one thousand and five hundred dollar price tag on his head. I was planning on cashing in on that reward as soon as we got to Las Cruces. I guess someone else will get it now, though," Dobbs said.

Dobbs didn't know it at the time, but Lomax was not the kind of man to let an opportunity slip by if it meant money in his pocket. If there was fifteen hundred dollars on a man's head, he wanted it; as long as the head it was on wasn't his that is.

"What's this hombre's name?" Lomax asked, trying to appear only mildly interested.

"Sackett...Brent Sackett; have you heard of him?" Dobbs asked.

Lomax thought for a few seconds before answering. Once he'd had a chance to consider the question he replied, "Yeah, I have. He shot a couple of lawmen if my memory serves me correctly."

"That reward might be even higher now," Dobbs went on seizing the moment and the opportunity. "That reward poster I have is several months old."

Lomax looked at Dobbs and nodded slightly. Lomax knew that none of his men could go to a local sheriff and claim the reward. If anyone did so it would have to be someone without a price on their own head. If this fella Dobbs was telling the truth he might be just the man to collect the reward and then hand it over to him.

"So, what is your proposal on this money?" Lomax asked as his eyes narrowed?

"All I want is five hundred dollars. I'll give you a thousand...I'll just hold out five hundred for myself," Dobbs said and paused before adding, "You need me to get the money and you know it."

"Hey, I don't need nobody for nothing," Lomax snapped angrily.

"None of your gang can go in and collect the reward money," Dobbs reiterated, knowing he was walking a fine line.

Lomax sat silent for a moment and then stood up and walked over to where Dobbs was tied. He looked down at Dobbs and slowly pulled his knife from its scabbard.

"If you're lying to me to save your miserable hide, hoss...I'll cut you from one end to the other. Do you hear me?"

"Yes, I hear you," Dobbs said and swallowed hard. "I ain't lying to you, though. Brent Sackett is camped right up there on that mountain," Dobbs said motioning towards the mountain behind Lomax.

"How many in this wagon train," Lomax asked?

"It ain't a wagon train. It's his wagon and mine. There's a young fella and his baby, and two kids whose folks were killed. Sackett has his woman with him. That's it. Like I said, there is no wagon train," Dobbs grinned.

"How far from here are they camped? We don't have a lot of time. I want to ride out early in the morning," Lomax stated.

"Even without this Slater fella you were talking about…the dynamite man?" Dobbs said indicating he was up on what was going on with the gang.

Lomax gave Dobbs another long hard stare. After careful consideration Lomax smiled.

"You're looking to join up with us, ain't you, hoss?" Lomax said with a slight nod.

"That I am, Lomax, that I am," Dobbs said with a grin. "I'm a valuable man to have around as you will see if you give me a try."

Lomax thought for a moment and could see that the gang might have some use for Dobbs; for the time being, anyway. Once he'd served his usefulness he could be disposed of easy enough.

Chapter
9

WITH SNAKE EYES BOB riding between them, Brian and AJ Sackett rode south staying on the Mexican side of the border. They felt it would be safer remaining on Mexican soil than running the risk that a posse might be looking for them for the shooting of Rawhide Deacon's brother.

Brian dropped back behind AJ and Bob to make sure they weren't being followed after the shoot out with the two members of the Mexican gang. After nearly five miles it was clear to Brian the gang had not given chase.

"We can take it easy," Brian said when he caught up to where AJ and Bob had stopped to wait for him. "There's no sign of anyone back behind us."

"Good, I don't want to wind our horses," AJ said.

Giving Bob a hard look AJ said tightly, "You don't know how much I want to kill you right now."

Brian gave his brother a quick glance, "AJ...," he warned, "...we need him."

"I know, I know...I'm not going to kill him. But, if a jury lets him off easy I'll hunt him down and do what needs to be done to a varmint like this," AJ said with a deep frown.

Brian looked at Bob and could see a look of concern in his eyes. He knew that given the chance

Bob would try and make a run for it. They'd have to be very careful not to give him that opportunity.

The three of them topped a rise and suddenly reined up. Off to their right, no more than three hundred yards were eight Comanche warriors. They were heading in the same direction as the Sacketts were.

"Do you see what I see?" Brian asked.

"I see 'em and I say let's lose 'em," AJ said, then looked at Bob and added. "You'd better keep up or I'm for letting them have you."

AJ knew that would keep Bob riding with them for the time being. He certainly wouldn't want to face the Comanches by himself. The three of them kicked their mounts into full runs.

Brian motioned for them to head towards the border. The Comanches had an angle on them if they rode straight and Brian wanted a lot of distance between them and the Indians.

The three of them rode hard over rise after rise; each time checking the whereabouts of the Indians. Every time they got a good fix on the Comanches they were giving chase and about the same distance away that they were when they first saw them.

When the three of them topped the highest ridge they looked down a long hill towards the Rio Grande River. On the other side they spotted several wagons on the US side of the border. This could be their salvation.

"Head for the river," Brian yelled as they headed down the long slope.

"You won't have to wait for me," AJ yelled back.

They were about fifty yards from the bottom of the hill when Bob's horse stumbled, spilling him over its head.

Between Heaven and Hell

Brian looked back and saw what had happened and reined his horse to a sliding halt. He reined it around and headed back up the hill. Just as he reached Bob the Comanches topped the hill and started down the slope firing their rifles.

Bob swung up on Brian's horse behind him, but a mere second later a bullet from a Comanche rifle hit him in the back. He fell hard against Brian but remained on the horse.

"Hang on Bob, this is going to be close," Brian said as he kicked his horse up again.

AJ stopped and opened fire on the Comanches which forced them to slow up. Brian made it to the river and as he rode out into it, Snake Eyes Bob fell from the horse. He was dead.

Brian started to stop and tend to Bob, but when he saw him floating face down in the water knew there was no use. AJ rode up to Brian who was staring down at Bob.

"He's dead, Brian," AJ said as he rode up alongside his brother.

The gunfire from the Comanches forced them to ride on towards the wagons they had seen from the hilltop. Once they reached them they figured the Comanches would turn back.

The two brothers rode hard leaning out over their horse's necks to make themselves smaller targets. The Comanches kept up their pursuit. Riding up to the first wagon Brian saw that the driver was a Mexican. The man had his rifle held to his shoulder, but wasn't firing at the approaching Comanches.

The man seated next to the Mexican was a Caucasian, but definitely a 'hard case'. AJ was peering over his shoulder at the Comanches and hadn't looked in the direction of the occupants of the wagon. It was only when he turned his attention back towards Brian that he became aware of who the men in the wagons were...they were Comancheros.

As Brian passed by the wagon, the Gringo aboard it swung his rifle and hit Brian in the head knocking him off his horse. Seeing this AJ shot the Gringo, killing him. The Mexican man driving the wagon pulled his pistol and started to fire at AJ. AJ swung his gun towards the Mexican, but before either man could fire AJ's horse tripped and fell, spilling him out over its head and rendering him unconscious.

Both Sackett brothers lay on the ground out cold as the Comanches rode up and surrounded them. The Indians remained on their horses and were soon joined by the Comancheros from the wagons. They all stared down at the two men who lay on the ground before them.

"Kill them," one of the Comanche warriors said.

"No, wait. Tie them up and put them in one of the wagons. We might have use for these men," one of the Comancheros said forcefully.

"I say they die," the Comanche snapped.

"And I say no. We may have need for them. You want more guns and ammunition and we need more money. I know this man," the Comanchero stated.

"His name is Brent Sackett," the Comanchero said mistakenly.

Chapter
10

BRENT SACKETT crept up to the thicket next to where Denver Dobbs was being held captive. Most of the outlaw gang had turned in for the night, but a few were still sitting around a campfire.

Brent surveyed the situation and saw that he could get within eight or nine feet of where Bob was bound hand and foot. However, he would have to expose himself to an open area in order to get to Dobbs to cut the ropes that had him bound.

Sam Lomax was sitting with another member of the gang, but had his back turned towards Dobbs. Lomax was still contemplating the fifteen hundred dollars Dobbs had told him about and was talking it over with Boles, his right hand man. The two were sharing a bottle of whiskey.

Brent looked heavenward and saw the clouds had moved into the area and would very shortly block the glow of the full moon, making it easier to reach Dobbs without being seen. It shouldn't be but a minute or two before the area would be much darker.

Manny Chavez walked over to where Lomax and Boles were seated and nodded towards them.

"Hey, boss...what about moving the woman over next to the hombre we have tied up over there. That way one man could keep his eyes on both of them?" Chavez offered.

Lomax turned and looked towards Dobbs and then back at Chavez.

"Yeah, go ahead. That's a good idea Chavez," Lomax said.

Brent heard what was said and knew this was going to make his job much harder now. He'd have to wait until the entire camp was asleep and then take out the gang member watching over the two prisoners.

All Brent could do now was wait! He didn't have to wait long, however, because one of the other gang members decided to relieve himself behind the thicket where Brent was hiding.

The Mexican man got up from where he had been seated by the campfire and walked in Lomax's direction. When he got to where Lomax, Boles, and Chavez were seated Lomax looked up at the man said something as the man passed which made the others laugh.

Brent hurriedly looked around and then pressed himself into the thorny thicket. Just as the gang member rounded the corner of the thicket, a cloud covered the moon casting a dark shadow over the land. It hid Brent from the man's view.

The man turned his back to where Brent was standing and started to relieve himself. Moving like a cat, Brent slipped up behind the man and grabbed him from behind, covering the man's mouth as he plunged his knife into the man's back.

The groan the man made didn't go unnoticed by Lomax and the others, but due to the man's reason for going behind the thicket they paid no attention to it. Brent quickly dragged the body up into the thicket where it would be much harder to spot.

Brent pulled the man's vest and sombrero off of him and put them on. As long as no one got a good look at his face they would just think it was the man he'd just killed.

Chavez, meanwhile, had gone over to escort Mrs. Keeling over to where Dobbs was being kept. Mrs. Keeling looked up at Chavez and caught the wink he gave her as he told the man guarding her, what Lomax had ordered.

"Good, hombre...you can watch her while I get some sleep," the man said as Chavez took Mrs. Keeling's hand and helped her to her feet.

"Over there," Chavez said gruffly, giving her a shove in order to make it appear he didn't like the woman.

Brent remained hidden behind the thicket, but knew he would have to be seen eventually to keep one of the gang from coming to check on the man he'd just killed.

Brent eyed the camp and noticed that there were a number of whiskey and tequila bottles being passed around. This was a blessing in disguise. It wouldn't be long before it would start to have an effect on the gang and that would make Brent's job a lot easier.

Chavez and Mrs. Keeling's arrival at the spot where Dobbs was being held made it possible for Brent to walk out from behind the thicket and take a seat in a shadowy area away from Lomax and the others. He immediately lay down pretending to go to sleep.

Dobbs looked surprised when he realized the person Chavez sat next to him was a woman. He looked at her quizzically and then at Chavez. He started to say something, but Chavez spoke first.

"Shh...Mrs. Keeling will explain everything to you. Listen to what she says and do exactly as she does when the time comes," Chavez whispered, causing Dobbs to sit up straighter. "Be ready to move."

With that Chavez moved away from them and sat down where the previous guard had been stationed. Chavez didn't know exactly how he was going to arrange for the man and woman's escape, but he knew when the time was right he would know.

Brent lay on his side so he could watch the entire camp. Once the last man went to sleep he'd make his move. He was hoping that the man guarding Dobbs and the woman would doze off, but that wasn't likely. As he lay there the clouds covered the moon.

Chapter
11

BRIAN AND AJ awoke bound hand and foot inside one of the Comancheros wagons. The jostling of the wagon told them they were either on a very rough road or traveling cross country. Brian looked towards the front of the wagon and saw that there was only one man seated on the bench.

His head ached terribly from the blow he'd suffered. AJ was in no better shape from the spill he'd taken when his horse fell. They looked at one another with serious expressions etched on their face, but then they both smiled. They were still alive, after all.

Brian whispered, "What happened anyway?"

"You almost had your head taken off with a rifle. My horse fell and sent me flying over its head. How do you feel?" AJ asked.

"Like someone tried to take my head off with a rifle. How do we get out of this mess?" Brian asked, looking down at the ropes.

"I'll have to think about that for a while. Can you move around so you can see out the back of the wagon?" AJ asked.

"I think so," Brian said and began trying to maneuver himself around so he could get a fix on the situation at hand.

It took some doing, but Brian finally was able to get in a position where he could look out the back. It was night, but there was a full moon which allowed him to see some distance.

There was another wagon behind the one they were in and a man on horseback riding along on each side of the last wagon. A woman sat alongside the man driving the wagon; it appeared that she too had her hands bound.

"Hey, there's a woman on the wagon behind us," Brian said.

"This is no time for you to start eyeballing some woman; we're in a real bind here," AJ said sounding serious.

"I didn't mean it that way, AJ. By the looks of it, she may be a prisoner, too. It looks like her hands are tied in front of her," Brian pointed out.

"These Comancheros have been known to kidnap women and take them to Mexico to be sold into slavery. If they're filling an order for some slave trader, I'll bet you a month's pay there are more," AJ commented.

Brian lay back down so his back was to AJ.

"Can you get your hands on these ropes I'm tied with?" Brian asked.

"Let me turn around; I think I might be able to," AJ answered.

The two jockeyed around until AJ's hands were in a position to fumble with the knot in Brian's rope. It was hard to figure out how to untie the knot since he was unable to see it; but, eventually he got it loosened.

Just as Brian felt the rope loosen on his hands the driver of the wagon they were in looked back at them.

"Hey...What are you two up to back there?" the man questioned.

"Just trying to get comfortable; you haven't missed a rut or hole yet," Brian replied.

"Shut up; you're lucky to be alive. The Comanches wanted to kill you," the man informed them.

"Oh, is that right? Who do we thank for our still being alive?" Brian asked, actually curious.

"Machete Perez...maybe you have heard of him?"

Brian looked at AJ who gave a slight shrug of his shoulder's indicating he had never heard the name before. Brian started to speak, but suddenly remembered seeing a wanted poster on Machete Perez the last time he was in Mexico.

"Yes, I have heard of him," Brian said, causing AJ to look at him questioningly.

"Everyone in these parts knows and fears the name, I can tell you that. Soon the Machete gang will be bigger than the James gang, the Younger Brothers, and the Dalton boys all together," the man boasted.

"Oh, why's that?" Brian said as he freed his hands completely.

"We are going to rob..., never mind that. You probably won't be around to see it, anyway," the man said glancing back at them again.

"So this Machete is going to save us from the Comanches so you Comancheros can kill us," Brian went on, stealing a quick look behind their wagon again.

"Something like that...yeah. I can tell you this I guess. You and the others are going to be some of the hostages killed to show we mean business when we get to where we are going," the man stated.

"Oh, where are we going? You can tell us that, can't you," Brian continued bending forward and starting to untie the ropes around his feet while keeping an eye on the driver's back?

"Yeah, I suppose so. We are going to Uvalde. There is a bank there with a lot of money in it just waiting for us to take it and run," the driver said, turning his head around, but not actually looking back towards Brian and AJ.

"You ain't going to get far trying to outrun a posse in these wagons," Brian answered; continuing to do all the talking.

"We ain't going to have to outrun no posse in these wagons. The money will be in the wagons, but the posse will be looking for men on horseback," the driver said with a chuckle.

"Oh, I see. Where is Machete at now," Brian asked?

"He's riding up ahead, him and five of the gang. He likes to scout ahead and not rely on someone else telling him what we're riding into," the man said, obviously impressed by Machete Perez.

"You said earlier that 'we' and the 'others' were going to be killed to show you mean business. Who are the others you were talking about," Brian said, getting the ropes untied from around his feet, but leaving the ropes over them to appear he was still bound?

"The couple in the wagon behind us; we will sacrifice one person a day until the money is turned over to us," the man stated.

"What if the town holds out longer than four days?" Brian asked.

"Then we actually start to kill one of the townspeople. Machete says that it won't take five days; maybe just three. Of course, the woman will be the third one to be killed. Machete says that is when the townspeople will give in."

"And you'd actually kill a woman, eh?" Brian said.

"Yeah…makes sense don't it."

"Why not just kill some kid on day one. That would really get them in the right frame of mind to give up the money," Brian said with a frown.

"Hey, we don't kill children. Something we will not do is to kill a child. If they happen to run in front of a bullet while we're making our getaway…that is a different story and cannot be helped."

"You're all heart," Brian said as he went to work on AJ's ropes while still being aware of the driver.

Just then one of the Comancheros rode up alongside the wagon and engaged the driver in conversation. This gave Brian plenty of time to concentrate on getting AJ freed. He had AJ's hands freed quickly. AJ then untied the ropes around his feet.

Now they were both freed from their bindings, but were still between a rock and a hard place. There were no guns in the back of the wagon; only the one on the driver and a rifle in the boot well. The next thing the Sacketts would need was a workable plan of escape.

Raymond D. Mason

Chapter

12

BRENT SACKETT lay watching the gang members as they all turned in for the night. It wouldn't be long before they'd all be asleep considering the amount of alcohol they'd consumed. The snoring soon testified to that.

Brent watched the man guarding Dobbs and the woman and tried to lay out a plan in sneaking up behind the man. It wouldn't be easy, but he'd have to try.

The slightest noise would alert the guard that he was being stalked; and if the full moon were to shine through the clouds Brent would be in the open and an easy target. As he watched the guard, however, he soon realized that there was something going on between him, Dobbs, and the woman. The guard was freeing them.

Brent watched as the guard cut the ropes and then led them quietly to where the horses were tethered. He helped the woman aboard a horse and then gave Dobbs a boost as well.

The way the guard kept looking back to where Lomax was sleeping told Brent that he wasn't part of the gang. If he wasn't part of the gang why was he with them? The only explanation for that was that he had something against one of the gang members, probably Lomax; or, he was a lawman of some kind.

Brent breathed a sigh of relief, knowing that he wouldn't have to attempt to free Dobbs. As far as the woman's captivity he hadn't really given it much thought.

Dobbs and the woman walked the horses away from the camp while Chavez moved back towards the spot where he had supposedly been standing guard. Brent wondered how this man would explain the fact that both prisoners escaped while he was on guard duty.

Brent had an idea. He'd give the man an alibi. He'd knock the guard out. That should satisfy Lomax and the others as to how the couple escaped. Now, if he could get close enough to the man without getting shot.

Chavez unwittingly made Brent's idea a lot easier; he walked back to within six feet of where Brent was laying and turned his back to take one last look towards Dobbs and Mrs. Keeling. Brent quickly, but quietly got to his feet and hit Chavez over the head with the butt of his pistol, knocking him out cold.

Brent quickly turned around and looked at the rest of the gang members in the camp to make sure they had not been aroused. When he saw they hadn't, he took a quick look in the direction that Dobbs and the woman had made good their escape. The night shadows had swallowed them up.

Moving silently Brent hurried to where the horses were tied and cut the tie rope of each horse. Brent swung upon the last horse he freed and began to herd the other horses away from the camp.

He knew the sound of the hoof beats would awaken some of the men, so he pulled his pistol and fired two shots into the air. That was all it took to spook the horses and awaken the entire camp.

Brent rode after the stampeding horses, leaning out over the neck of the horse he was riding. Shots began to ring out from the gang members. He could hear shouts of "He's stampeded the horses...get 'em."

Brent kept yelling and spooking the runaway horses so it would take the gang the rest of the night at least to catch up to them; if even then. This had worked out better than Brent had hoped for.

Meanwhile, back in the camp Lomax found the unconscious Chavez and figured that whoever had freed the captives had knocked Chavez out in order to do so.

Lomax sent several members of his gang after the horses while he tried to revive Chavez. When Chavez finally regained consciousness he touched the back of his head and winced.

"Someone hit me over the head," Chavez said groggily.

"Yeah, I can see that. It must have been the one we saw riding away and spooking our horses. You didn't get a look at the man," Lomax quizzed?

"No, I was sitting there watching the two when all of a sudden...bang; and I went out like a light."

Lomax moved Chavez's hand and felt the knot on the back of Chavez's head.

"Ouch," Chavez said at the roughness of Lomax's touch.

"You got yourself a good sized goose egg there, Chavez," Lomax said stifling a grin.

"I hope I do, considering this headache I've got. So the prisoner's were helped to escape, huh?" Chavez said acting surprised.

"Yeah...you didn't see anyone?" Lomax questioned.

"No, I didn't. Everything was as quiet as a church house on Monday morning. Are we missing any men?" Chavez asked.

"I don't know yet. I can tell you this, though. I will not rest until I find the one who did this. And I think I might know his name," Lomax said and paused before saying, "I'll find him and when I do I will kill him."

Chapter

13

MACHETE PEREZ stood smiling through the back of the wagon at Brian and AJ. He paced back and forth as he eyed them without speaking. Finally he stopped and spoke.

"You...you killed one of my men," Machete said as he frowned at AJ. "I don't like people shooting my men."

AJ gave Machete a long hard stare but didn't reply. Machete nodded his head slowly and then a grin slowly spread over his face.

"But...you did me a favor when you killed that man. I was going to do it myself. He was a thief," Machete said going from smile to a surprised expression.

"Aren't all Comancheros thieves?" AJ replied.

"Si...but we don't steal from each other. He stole from that man over there," Machete said and paused before saying, "So we will kill you quickly."

"You're all heart," AJ responded which got a laugh from Machete.

"It is too bad you must die, because I think I like you," Machete said.

"That's the thrill of a lifetime," AJ added.

Again Machete laughed and said, "I will kill you myself to make sure you do not suffer too much."

Machete, standing on the outside of the wagon could not tell that the two brothers had the ropes that had bound them merely wrapped loosely around their feet and hands. They were just waiting for the right moment to make a move to escape.

"Bring the other two prisoners out here," Machete called to his men, turning his back on Brian and AJ.

One of his men went to one of the other wagons and dragged a man and a woman out and stood them in front of Machete.

The man was slightly built and looked like he might be a bookkeeper or accountant. The woman was beautiful. She had long dark hair and appeared to be in her mid twenties. Brian looked quickly at AJ and grinned approvingly.

"Is that the one you saw earlier," AJ whispered?

"Yeah, but I couldn't see her face real clear. She's beautiful," Brian said honestly.

Machete was standing no more than five feet from the back of the wagon Brian and AJ were in, and totally focused on the woman.

"Why did you take such a beautiful woman," Machete asked the man standing with the couple?" He then quickly added, "You should have taken an ugly woman so we would not regret what we have to do."

Brian looked at AJ as he removed the ropes from his hands and feet. AJ nodded slightly and did the same. Once they were totally free from their bindings they surveyed the surroundings.

The horses were all tied to a tethering line and saddled. Once they made their move they'd have to move quickly to get the drop on all the men present.

That meant knowing where every man was when they made that move.

AJ counted the men as did Brian. Once they'd accounted for all they could see, AJ flashed the number on his fingers and got an agreeing nod from Brian.

Brian whispered so only AJ could hear him, "On three."

AJ nodded and Brian started the countdown, "One, two...three."

On the count of three both men leaped from the back of the wagon, landing on the ground behind Machete. Brian grabbed the leader of the Comancheros around the neck and grabbed one of the two pistols Machete was wearing from its holster. AJ grabbed the second pistol.

"Hold it right there or he dies," Brian yelled at the stunned gang members.

AJ's eyes darted quickly from one man to the next. Their move had caught the Comancheros by total surprise and no one had been able to draw their weapon.

Brian held the pistol under Machete's chin and called to the couple that was being held captive.

"Over here, quick," Brian ordered.

The man and woman wasted no time in moving from where they had been standing to the side of AJ. Machete held still since Brian had cocked the hammer back on the pistol. Machete knew that the gun had a hair trigger.

"Be careful, Amigo. That gun has a very sensitive trigger," Machete said quietly and evenly.

"Then you'd better not struggle in the least," Brian replied.

"I won't. But you cannot get away from here," Machete said.

"We'll see about that," Brian replied. "All of you drop your guns and back up," he ordered.

The men looked at one another and then slowly obeyed the order. AJ and the timid acting little man; at AJ's urging; moved around picking up the Comancheros' weapons. Once they had gathered them all up they dropped them into the water barrel on the side of the wagon where AJ and Brian had been held captive earlier.

AJ didn't hesitate in making his next move. He ordered the little man to keep the gang covered while he got four horses from the tethering line. He cut all but the four horses they would use loose and spooked the others. AJ untied the four horses they would be riding and mounted up. He led the other three to where Brian and the woman and man were waiting.

Unbeknownst to Brian and AJ, Machete had sent one of his men, Pablo Cerritos, out to scout the surrounding area for the best route to follow on towards Uvalde. Cerritos topped a ridge that allowed him to see what was going on where the wagons had stopped.

Cerritos rode his horse behind a rock formation and quickly climbed atop it while staying well hidden from view of those in the camp. He quickly discerned what was taking place and tried to figure out what he might be able to do.

Slowly a smile spread across Cerritos' face. He and Machete had been at odds several times and he found he enjoyed seeing the man humiliated like this. He knew exactly what his course of action would be...nothing.

He would let Machete's humiliation remain and not say, or do, a thing about it. After all he had been sent out of the camp to find the best route to Uvalde.

As Cerritos watched from his perch atop the rocks a thought crossed his mind. If he were to try and break this escape attempt up it would not be inconceivable that a stray bullet might find its way into Machete's heart. That would open the door for him to become the leader of the gang.

The rift between Machete and Cerritos had developed over a spilled bottle of Tequila. Cerritos had accidentally kicked over the uncorked bottle while passing by Machete and about one third of it had spilled out.

That was all it took to set Machete off and he jumped to his feet and struck Cerritos with a leather quirt. The sting had long since passed, but not the thought of Machete's action.

Cerritos had vowed to himself that one day he would kill Machete for what he'd done. He had never voiced his solemn vow to another living soul, but the incident had remained in the back of his mind. This could very well be the day vengeance was served.

Cerritos was well within rifle range and there was nothing between Machete and him but open space. He grabbed his rifle from its scabbard and lay down on a rock so he could hold a steady bead on his target.

Cerritos cocked the hammer back on the Winchester and took careful aim. He didn't want to make it obvious that his target was Machete, so he'd have to wait until just the right moment to fire. It came quickly.

Machete moved away from Brian just enough to make it look like a shot intended for the tall Texan missed and hit the gang leader. Cerritos slowly squeezed the trigger. Just as the hammer fell, Machete dropped a piece of rope he had been holding and bent over to pick it up.

The bullet from Cerritos' rifle passed over Machete's head and hit one of the other Comancheros in the shoulder. The man let out a scream and fell to the ground.

The gunshot also caused enough confusion and panic to send some of the Comancheros scrambling for cover. Machete, however, looked in the direction the shot had come from and spotted Cerritos some two hundred yards away.

AJ and the man and woman had already mounted up and AJ rode up to where Brian stood leading Brian's horse. Brian swung into the saddle and the four of them kicked their mounts into a full run while Machete and the others rushed towards the wagon where AJ had deposited their guns.

Machete stood and watched the four riders disappear over a rise and knew it would be useless to try and catch them. The first thing he did was order some of the men to go and round up the horses. The second thing he did was glare in the direction of the rocks where Cerritos had been when he tried to kill him.

Chapter

14

BRENT SACKETT rode to the spot where Julia and the others were waiting with the wagons and was pleased, yet surprised, to see Dobbs and Mrs. Keeling there as well.

"I see you found the wagons," Brent said as he slid off the back of the horse he'd been riding bareback.

"It was by accident, I can tell you that," Dobbs said with a grin. After a pause he added, "I owe you big time...Brent," he said sincerely. "And I do mean 'big time'."

Brent grinned slightly and nodded his head affirmatively, "I gotcha, Dobbs. Think nothing of it."

"I'll never know how to thank you, sir," Mrs. Keeling said with a wide smile. After getting a head nod from Brent she went on, "That man guarding us actually helped us escape. I don't think he was really a part of the gang; at least he said he wasn't."

"Is that right?" Brent asked questioningly.

"That's the way it looked and sounded to me," Dobbs added.

Brent shook his head, "I hope I didn't hit him too hard when I knocked him out. I'd hate to think I injured the man who was helping you out of that tight spot."

Brent paused and then asked, "How did you wind up with that gang, anyway?"

"It's a long story, so I'll give you the short version," she said. "My husband and I, along with two other families were on our way to Tucson, Arizona when we were attacked by the gang. They killed my husband and the other two men, but held us women captive.

"I heard they were going to sell us to a man who runs a string of...prostitutes...up to the mining camps. About eight of the gang members took the other two women and split off from the gang down there," she said motioning in the direction of Lomax and the others.

"The leader of the gang, Lomax is his name; liked me and wanted me to remain with him and the other members. I don't know exactly what his plan for me was, but I must say he didn't bother me at all. That's the crux of the story," Mrs. Keeling stated.

"I've heard of men who run women up to the mining camps; they're scum as far as I'm concerned," Brent said with a frown and then checked the sky.

"Let's get loaded up. If we're going to get by that bunch down there, now is the time to do it. They're on foot...at least most of them are. When we go through that camp I'll add a little insult to injury," Brent said as he looked at Grant and grinned.

They began to load up with Brent assigning people to the two wagons. He wanted the baby and the kids with him and Julia. He told Grant to ride with Dobbs and told him what he wanted him to do with two sticks of the dynamite they'd found in the gang members saddlebags.

"Grant, you follow my lead," Brent said firmly. "When you see me throw that first stick of dynamite, I want you to do the same.

"Dobbs, you stay right behind me and follow me wherever I go. If they've got something blocking our way I'll see it first and lead you around it," Brent said evenly.

Once they were loaded and ready to go Brent gave the order to move out. He held the team back as they descended the steep mountain slope. When they got within three hundred yards of where the gang had been camped, however, Brent whipped the team of horses into a full run.

Dobbs followed along behind Brent with Grant riding in the back of the wagon. When they got to within two hundred yards of the campsite Brent handed the reins to Julia and climbed into the back of the wagon where he quickly lit the fuse on a stick of dynamite.

As the two wagons rolled through the campsite Brent threw the first stick of dynamite in the direction of a number of gang members who had started firing at the wagons. No sooner had Brent's stick of dynamite exploded; sending a huge cloud of dust into the morning sky, than Grant's dynamite blew as well.

Only four of the gang member's horses had been rounded up by the gang since Brent had spooked them earlier. The two explosions spooked the already skittish horses causing them to break free and bolt away again. One gang member, who had been holding one of the horse's lead ropes, lost his footing and was dragged by the horse until he finally let go of the rope.

Lomax yelled for the men to let the wagons go. He was more concerned about rounding up the horses they'd lost and getting on to Las Cruces than trying to do anything about the wagons.

Brent climbed back onto the driver's bench with Julia and took the harness reins. He looked at her and she gave him a very weak smile. Brent did a double take and that's when he noticed the spot of blood that was slowly spreading and getting larger in the rib cage area of her jacket.

"You've been hit, Julia," Brent said with a deep look of concern spreading across his face.

"It's nothing, Brent," Julia said; then forced a smile and slumped over, resting her head on his shoulder.

Brent put his right arm around her and held her close to him as the team of horses raced on down the trail. He couldn't stop to tend to Julia's wound; not so close to the gang's camp. All he could do was keep the horses running as fast as they could. He found himself doing something else, also...praying a silent prayer.

Chapter
15

BRENT PULLED back hard on the harness reins and brought the team of horses to a halt. He quickly lifted Julia's limp body into the back of the wagon and began trying to stop the bleeding.

Obviously one of the shots fired by the gang had hit her as they rode past their camp. Dobbs pulled his wagon up alongside Brent's and Dobbs called out to him.

"What is it Brent...why did you pull up?"

"Julia's been hit. I have to try and stop the bleeding," Brent yelled back.

Mrs. Keeling heard what was said and instantly offered her assistance.

"I am a nurse. Let me take a look at her," Mrs. Keeling said as she climbed down off Dobbs' wagon.

Cheryl Keeling wasted no time in attending to the serious wound in Julia's side. The bullet had ricocheted off a rib and was lodged in Julia's intestines. There was probably more bleeding internally than externally. The wound was life threatening and Mrs. Keeling knew it.

"She's hurt very bad," Mrs. Keeling said after having looked at the wound.

"Can you stop the bleeding?" Brent asked.

"It's more than just that, I'm afraid. There's no exit wound so the bullet is lodged inside her and there's no way of telling how much damage has been done. We have to get her to a doctor," Mrs. Keeling said with a pained look on her face.

Brent looked at Julia with a deep concern on his face and then it turned to pleading when he turned his attention to Mrs. Keeling.

"Can't you do anything?" he asked in a pained voice.

"No...she needs to be operated on. Anything we tried to do like that out here would simply hasten her...her death," Mrs. Keeling said, being as truthful as she possibly could.

"Oh God...don't let her die," Brent said under his breath.

"How far are we from Las Cruces?" Mrs. Keeling asked.

"I don't know...fifteen; twenty miles, I guess," Brent said gazing fixedly down at Julia's pretty face.

"We've got to get her there as fast as we can, then," Mrs. Keeling stated.

"What about a doctor coming out here?" Brent questioned and then added, "It would be a lot faster by horseback."

"I'm not sure if a doctor could even operate out here, but that would be the fastest way. If I have things set up here as best as I can for an operation...yes, yes...a doctor could operate out here," Mrs. Keeling said pondering the idea.

"I'll ride ahead and bring a doctor back. I'll have him bring everything he'll need to do the operation here in the wagon," Brent said with a sound of excitement in his voice.

"If you can find one who is willing to make the trip, it will be faster. We'll continue on towards Las Cruces naturally; so you won't have as far to go on the return trip," Mrs. Keeling said thoughtfully.

"I'll leave now," Brent said and started to stand up, but paused for a moment and looked down at Julia. He knelt down beside her and kissed her lips tenderly.

"Hang on, honey. Help is on the way," he whispered.

He got up and climbed out the back of the wagon. Grant Holt had climbed out of Dobbs' wagon and was standing looking in where Julia lay.

"I'm taking your horse, Grant. I've got to get a doctor," Brent stated.

"I know, I heard. Go with God's speed, Brent," Grant said.

Brent ran to where Grant's horse was tied to the back of Dobbs' wagon; he untied it and swung into the saddle. He kicked the horse into a full run down the trail.

As Grant and Dobbs watched Brent ride away Grant said, "We'd better keep moving. That gang may gather their horses and be coming after us."

"I doubt they'll have an easy time rounding up those horses after that dynamite display," Dobbs said with a grin and then added, "But you're right. We'd better keep moving."

"Do you want to take the lead?" Grant asked.

"No, you take the lead since that's the wagon with Mrs. Sackett in it. I'll bring up the rear," Dobbs said agreeably and then added. "The kids can ride with me so Mrs. Keeling will have more room with Mrs. Sackett."

Grant looked at Dobbs with a new found appreciation. This was the first time he'd shown any concern for anyone other than himself. Perhaps this ordeal had some good in it after all, Grant thought to himself.

Brent rode hard for over an hour. When he felt the horse begin to weaken he feared he had pushed it too hard. It was only then that he slowed to give it a breather.

The more Brent thought of the possibility of losing Julia the more his heart ached. If she was to die he didn't know what he would do. The thought was almost too much for him to endure. If she did die he wouldn't rest until he'd killed every member of Sam Lomax's gang; starting with Lomax himself.

The sky overhead had a few scattered clouds which bothered Brent. The last thing he wanted was for it to rain and make traveling that much more difficult. He patted the neck of Grant's horse and said, "Sorry, boy, but we've got to go."

Fortunately the trail became a little easier and Brent resisted the urge to get too much out of the horse. He kept it at an easy lope which allowed the animal to gradually get its wind back.

Brent had traveled a good ten miles when he met a cavalry patrol. When they saw him the captain in charge raised his hand and called his troops to a halt. Brent rode up to where they were and his heart quickened.

A man wearing a tan duster had a medical bag attached to the side of his saddle. He was a cavalry doctor. Brent felt his prayers had been answered. He reined up in front of the captain and smiled widely.

"Man, am I glad to see you, Captain. My wife has been shot and needs a doctor something terrible. I see you have an army doctor along with you," Brent gushed forth.

"Where is your wife?" the captain asked.

"She's about ten miles back on the trail. We ran across a gang led by Sam Lomax and they shot at us; that is how she got wounded," Brent said.

"Lomax, huh," the captain said. "We're on the trail of several renegade Apaches who escaped from custody," the captain said as he turned in the saddle and looked at the doctor.

"Hey, Doc, did you hear what this man said?" the captain asked.

"Yes, I did. Why don't we follow the renegades' trail as far as we can and when they turn off the main trail I'll go and take a look at this man's wife? You can have one of the troopers go with me and then we'll catch up to you," the doctor offered.

"That's all right with me. Let's go then. Forward, ho," the captain said and the troopers, led by Brent, headed back in the direction of the wagons and Julia.

The troopers held a steady pace; nothing as torrid as the one Brent had been keeping. His horse was able to rest a bit more at the reduced speed. Hopefully the doctor would be able to do something about the bullet lodged in Julia's stomach.

Brent had high hopes because of the 'field doctoring' the army physicians were used to performing. At least it would be a real medical doctor looking after Julia and not someone without any real medical experience.

They had traveled about five miles when the Apache's horses' tracks left the main trail and cut cross country. The cavalry patrol followed the Indian's trail and the doctor and a corporal went on with Brent.

It took close to an hour and a half for Brent and the other two men to reach the wagons from the time Brent had met up with the cavalry detail. As they approached the wagons that had stopped Brent noticed instantly the somber looks on everyone's face.

"What is it...?" Brent asked as he rode up to where Grant Holt and Mrs. Keeling were standing.

Grant cast a quick glance at Mrs. Keeling and then up at Brent and said quietly, "She's gone, Brent."

Brent's face turned a pale shade of gray at the words as he leaped from the horse he was riding.

"What... gone..., where is she?" Brent said with a stunned look on his face.

Grant looked at the wagon where Julia's body was, but didn't speak. Brent rushed to the back of the wagon and peered in. Julia was lying there with her hands folded across her bosom.

She looked so peaceful; like she was sleeping. There was even a slight smile on her lips. Brent felt a spear of pain shoot from his heart and go through his entire body and weakening his knees, as he slowly climbed into the wagon.

He gently touched Julia's cheek with his fingertips. Her skin felt cool, almost cold. He closed his eyes and turned his face upwards as he let out a low, painful groan.

Julia was gone. He'd never see her again; not in this life. How could he go on without the only woman he'd ever loved? His love for Julia was what had changed him; now she was gone.

Tears burned in his eyes as he felt the lump in his throat grow large, almost cutting off his wind. He swallowed hard to try and force it away, but it remained. Finally he was unable to hold back the pain and sense of loss any longer and a torrent of tears burst forth.

Brent wept over Julia's body for a good ten minutes. The others moved away from the wagon to give him as much time as he needed to deal with his loss. They could still hear his sobs, though, and felt a deep sorrow for him.

Raymond D. Mason

Chapter
16

BRIAN SACKETT rode away from AJ and the other two to the top of a hill so he could check the trail behind them. There was no sign of the Comancheros. He grinned slightly as he galloped back down the hill and joined the three waiting for him.

"No sign of them," Brian said as he rode up to the trio.

"You'll never know how much I thank you for your bravery," the woman said with a stunning smile.

Brian blushed slightly, "It was nothing," he replied.

"I did most of the brain work," AJ said, getting a chuckle from Brian.

"Then I thank you too," the woman smiled again.

"What are your names, by the way?" AJ asked.

"I'm Terrin Gibbons. I was on my way to San Antonio when the Comancheros attacked the hired coach I was in. This man was also in the coach," Terrin explained.

"What's your name?" AJ asked.

"I'm Homer Timmons; I'm an auditor and was on my way to audit the books at one of the banks in San Antonio. Miss Gibbons and I were sharing the cost of the private coach," Timmons said wide eyed.

"I see. My name is AJ Sackett and this is my brother, Brian. Glad to make your acquaintance," AJ said with a slight grin.

"Not nearly as glad as we are, I can assure you," Terrin said sincerely.

"Oh, I don't know about that," Brian replied, obviously smitten by the woman's good looks.

"What do we do now?" Terrin asked.

"Well, let's see. You said you were headed for San Antonio, right?" Brian asked.

"Yes, that's right," Terrin replied.

"Then we'll see to it that you get there safely before we head back to our ranch up north," Brian said.

"That's awfully nice of you. I hope we're not being too much trouble?" Terrin answered.

"No...no trouble at all," Brian said and looked at AJ. "Ain't that right, AJ?"

"Yeah, that's right," AJ said with a grin as he gave Brian a quick glance.

"Where were you coming from when the Comancheros grabbed you?" AJ then asked.

"I had been to visit my fiancé in El Paso and was on my way back to a small town just north of San Antonio when we were attacked," Terrin said, causing Brian's smile to fade quickly.

"Your fiancé," he said quietly.

"I guess I should say my ex-fiancé. We broke off our engagement," Terrin said sadly.

Brian's grin returned as he said, "You did?"

"Yes, it seems he has a roving eye," Terrin answered.

"Well, that leaves you out, little brother," AJ said with a chuckle that got a glare from Brian.

"Nobody asked you. Don't pay any attention to him; he's just acting like a bothersome brother," Brian said apologetically.

Terrin smiled knowingly.

"What about you, Mr. Timmons; where were you coming from?" AJ continued to question.

"Oh, uh, I was coming from El Paso, also," Timmons said haltingly while looking nervously from Brian to AJ and then to Miss Gibbons.

"And you were going to San Antonio to audit a bank's books?" AJ said seriously.

"Yes, yes, that's right," Timmons said quickly.

There was something about Timmons that AJ didn't like, but he couldn't put his finger on it. The Comanchero driving the wagon they had been held in had told them where the gang was headed and that they were going to rob a bank that was busting at the seams with money. Who better than a bank auditor could give them information like that?

It could be the Comancheros had learned the information after they had captured the timid acting little man, but what if he was one of them? AJ would keep a close eye on Mr. Timmons.

They reined their horses in the direction of San Antonio and began the long journey northeastward. Brian kept his eyes on Terrin Gibbons while AJ kept a wary eye on Homer Timmons. It didn't take long before he spotted something a little troublesome about the little man.

AJ rode behind the other three mainly so he could keep an eye on Timmons. Although Timmons tried hard to hide it, his effort to leave a trail was spotted by AJ.

AJ decided to wait until they'd stopped to make camp before confronting Timmons with the fact that he knew what he was doing. He had also worked out a way to deal with the little auditor, or whatever he was, from that point on. Timmons would simply be bound hand and foot during the night. During the day he would ride with his hands tied together in front of him.

Meanwhile, Brent tossed the last shovel full of dirt on Julia's grave which was about fifty yards off the trail to Las Cruces. The others stood by solemnly watching Brent and wondering what he would do now.

Would he go on to California as originally planned, or would he change his mind and head somewhere else? What would happen to them? They had thought they would have a home with Brent and Julia, but now she was gone.

After tossing the last shovel full of dirt on the grave, Brent gently tapped down the entire grave. It was almost as though he didn't want to stop working on the grave because it would bring an end to his relationship with Julia.

Finally Brent stopped tamping down the grave and bowed his head. He stood there for several minutes not saying a word. When he had silently paid his final respects to his wife, he turned and pulled his hat down on his head.

"We can go now. Our next stop will be Las Cruces. From there...I really don't know where I'll be going, but it won't be on to California," he said firmly.

Everyone could see the change in Brent. There was no more smile. He took on a stern, almost angry look. The furrow between his eyes seemed to become a permanent fixture. He was also very short tempered.

As he started to climb aboard the wagon that had been his and Julia's he looked over at Dobbs with a fixed stare. Dobbs noticed and stood by his wagon waiting for Brent to say something.

After a few tortured seconds Brent said, "Dobbs if you are thinking about that reward I just want you to know that you'll never live long enough to spend it."

Dobbs could see the hate in Brent's eyes as he spoke the words. The truth was that Dobbs had already decided to drop the idea of turning Brent in to the law. He owed him for saving him from Lomax's gang and couldn't go through with his original plan.

Grant Holt was perplexed over Brent's decision. He'd left his small farm to follow Brent and Julia and the fact that Julia had taken such good care of his little daughter left him feeling helpless and hopeless.

Mrs. Keeling could see the pain in Brent's eyes and she had seen enough during her years as a nurse to know full well what he was going through. Right now he felt totally alone. He felt as if part of himself had died and was buried in that grave with Julia. There was bitterness and anger; anger at life; at God; and definitely at the ones responsible for her death.

She didn't know Brent all that well, having just met him; but, she knew his kind of man. He would go in search of the ones responsible. If he could he would attach his anger to the leader of the gang, but anyone having been a part of the gang would taste his revenge.

Mrs. Keeling, too, had lost a loved one; her husband. She was hurting and felt vulnerable; but due to her being taken captive had not had time to fully deal with her loss.

She had left her family behind in Tennessee when she and her husband had married and moved to Texas. She could always go back home, but things had changed there too. Her mother and father had been killed in a house fire a year after she left. She was alone now and very unsettled. Still, she felt for what Brent was going through.

Chapter 17

HOMER TIMMONS looked at AJ with a questioning look. He shook his head negatively as he responded to AJ's accusation.

"No, I'm not connected to the Comancheros," Timmons said in a whining voice. "I don't know what you thought you saw, but I can guarantee you that you must be mistaken."

"How can you say that, Timmons? You dropped clues every twenty or thirty yards. I found these beads in your coat pocket when you went to gather wood for the fire," AJ stated showing him a handful of beads.

"What about that Mr. Timmons?" Brian questioned as well.

"That was for me. In case we had to backtrack we'd have a trail to follow," Timmons said defensively.

"Why would we want to go back towards the Comancheros, Homer?" AJ snapped. "No, it was either for them to follow us; or, for you to find your way back to them."

"You heard what they had planned to do to us. They were going to sacrifice us to force the town to pay a ransom before they started killing residents of Uvalde," Timmons argued.

"How'd they know that bank was brimming over with money, huh? Wouldn't a bank auditor be able to tell them that?" AJ went on.

"I can assure you that I have a sterling record with the bank I work for. I've been with them for ten years and no one has ever questioned my honesty," Timmons said with a frown.

"Maybe they should have. I'll tell you what we're going to do. We'll take you on to San Antonio alright, but when we get there we're going to let the sheriff do a little checking up on you," AJ said.

"Now that you mention it," Terrin Gibbons said thoughtfully, "Mr. Timmons was in quite a hurry to get to San Antonio. And he spent a lot of time being questioned by Machete. And twice when they brought him back to the wagon where they were keeping us I could smell alcohol on his breath."

"They forced me to drink it. They said it would loosen my tongue," Timmons replied quickly.

"We'll see. If you have nothing to hide, then, there's nothing to worry about," AJ said with a grin. "But, there'll be no more laying a trail for you...or them, whichever the case might have been."

Las Cruces, NM

The two wagons rolled slowly down the main street through Las Cruces until they came to the sheriff's office. Brent pulled the team of horses to a halt and sat staring down at the ground, but not saying a word for several seconds.

Finally he looked at Mrs. Keeling who was seated next to him on the wagon's bench seat and said, "I'm sure the sheriff will want to hear all about your ordeal and that Sam Lomax and his gang might be headed this way. I'm glad we were able to help get you away from them."

"I'm so sorry about your wife. I didn't have a chance to really get to know her, but from what little I saw of her she seemed like a wonderful person," she said in a sincere voice.

"She was that all right. I don't think she had a mean bone in her body. One thing is for sure; she held my heart in her hands and took very good care of it. She was something very special to me," Brent said and then climbed down off the wagon to help Mrs. Keeling down.

Just as he took her hand while she climbed down the door to the sheriff's office opened and the sheriff stepped out onto the boardwalk. He eyed the two wagons questioningly and walked over to where Brent and Mrs. Keeling were standing.

"Howdy, folks...are you just passing through or planning on staying a while?" the sheriff asked.

"Just passing through," Brent said. "I think you ought to hear what this woman has to say to you, Sheriff. You may have big trouble headed this way."

"Oh...and how's that?" the sheriff asked with a frown.

"She'll explain it all to you," Brent said and then looked at Mrs. Keeling. "I'll be leaving you all here. You and Grant can have the wagon and decide what you're going to do. I'll be riding on alone from here."

Mrs. Keeling looked soulfully at Brent and said, "May God go with you."

"He deserted me a long time ago, I'm afraid."

"What is this 'trouble' all about that you say we have coming our way?" the sheriff cut in.

Brent looked sternly at him and said, "Sam Lomax."

With those final words Brent walked back to where Grant Holt was waiting on his horse and looked up at him.

"Grant...you take good care of yourself and that baby. Julia loved that little girl like she was her very own. I wish you all the luck in the world," Brent said evenly without showing much emotion.

Grant nodded his head slowly, "I guess I'll be staying right here in Las Cruces for awhile. I really don't have any plans since you're not going on to California."

"You do whatever you think is right. Adios my friend," Brent said as he untied his horse from the back of the wagon.

Dobbs was still seated on his wagon which was directly behind Brent's. He didn't say anything, merely sat in silence watching the goings on. Brent looked at him through a slight frown and said, "Dobbs...take care."

Dobbs nodded, "You too, Brent. I wish you were going on to California."

Brent didn't say anything as he climbed up on his horse and looked at the Thurston kids, Hank and Annie who were riding in the back of his wagon. They both wore sad looks mixed with some fear and uncertainty.

"Kids, you can go on with Grant wherever it is he's going. I can't go on with you. I've got something that I have to do and I have to do it alone. You'll be all right; Grant's a good man," Brent said, sensing their disappointment.

"We're sorry about...well, about everything," Hank said sadly.

Brent nodded his head knowingly, "I know Hank. Take care of your sister and maybe we'll run into each other again some time."

"I hope so," Hank said.

"I don't want you to go," Annie said as she cuddled her rag doll to her shoulder.

"I have to, honey. Hank will take good care of you. Bye," Brent said and forced a smile.

They all watched Brent as he reined his horse around and headed back down the street in the direction from which they'd just come. Brent had a date with fate and he didn't want to keep it waiting. Sam Lomax was somewhere behind them and Brent was going to find him if it was the last thing he ever did.

Raymond D. Mason

Chapter 18

SAM LOMAX stepped up on his horse and looked around at the other members of his gang. He wore a deep, angry frown as he called out, "Let's ride. Our next stop is Las Cruces and we're going to burn that town to the ground."

Lomax was still angry at the delay because of the scattering of their horses. They'd finally rounded them all up, but now they were far behind the schedule they had planned.

The dynamite man he'd expected had obviously been waylaid. The dynamite was used instead by the ones in the wagons when they rode past and scattered the horses. Lomax would like nothing better than to get his hands on the one or ones responsible for this. Little did he know that the man was riding back towards them!

The gang headed on down the trail towards Las Cruces with Lomax riding in front. Several of his men still had ringing in their ears from being too close to the dynamite blasts when they went off.

The gang rode at an even pace, keeping their horses in a slow, easy lope. Lomax could still see a blurry image in his mind's eye of the man who had thrown the first stick of dynamite from the lead wagon. He felt he'd recognize him if he ever saw him again.

Meanwhile, Brent was holding a steady pace heading back in Lomax's direction. Brent didn't care that he was vastly outnumbered. All he wanted to do was kill the man who had taken his Julia away from him. He blamed Sam Lomax for it.

It wasn't as if Brent had a death wish now, all he wanted was to seek retribution for Julia's death. Of course, if it meant losing his life to get his revenge, then so be it. He really didn't feel he had much to live for anyway.

The miles passed quickly. Brent saw the gang before they saw him and reined his horse off the trail and into a small stand of trees. He climbed off his mount and pulled his long gun out of the saddle scabbard.

As the leader of the gang Lomax would be riding in front of the others. There were two men taking the lead, however, as they approached. One of the men was a Mexican wearing a large sombrero, and the other man was a Gringo. Lomax would have to be the Gringo.

Brent picked a spot on the trail where he would open fire when the gang reached it. It would be an easy kill for him; no more than one hundred yards away from his position.

He tied his horse out of harm's way because of the hasty retreat he would have to make once he'd killed Lomax. There would be lead flying all over the stand of trees. Brent licked his thumb and then wiped the rifle's front sight with it to cut down on the glare.

The gang rode closer and closer to the kill point Brent had picked. As they neared the spot, Brent cocked the hammer back on the rifle. He leveled the rifle on the exact spot he'd picked to make his shot. Now all he could do was to wait.

The gang was only twenty to twenty five yards from the kill point when Lomax held up his hand for them to stop. The gang all reined up and waited to find out why he'd stopped them. It was soon very obvious to them all. It was the same cavalry patrol that Brent had run into earlier.

The trail of the renegade Indians the cavalry detail had been following had led them in a large circle right back to the main trail. Lomax didn't want a run in with the cavalry; not then; they'd already lost too much time.

"Every one get off the trail," he yelled out. "Take to the rocks and trees."

Lomax and the Mexican riding alongside him headed for a rock formation as the others scattered; taking to either the rocks or trees. Brent couldn't believe how they all just seemed to disappear.

Just as the cavalry detail reached the main trail, gunfire erupted from the underbrush. Troopers began falling from their mounts while others opened fire towards the brush. One after another the cavalrymen fell until all of them; including the doctor; had been shot.

Brent looked on in stunned disbelief. Once the shooting had stopped the Indians rode off in a cloud of dust; whopping and hollering as they rode away.

Brent realized he had passed right by the Apaches. That could very well be him lying on the ground out there. Of course, the Indians had laid the trap for the cavalry; not one lone rider.

It didn't take long for Lomax and his gang to show them-selves again once the shooting had stopped and the Apaches had fled. Lomax and the man who'd been riding alongside him earlier emerged from their hiding place first.

They were a good two hundred yards away and Brent didn't want to take a chance at missing his target from this far away. He'd wait until they got to the kill point he'd picked out. Lomax didn't have long for this world.

Again, Brent took aim on the spot he wanted Lomax in when he dropped the hammer on him. This time there was no distraction. Lomax and the Mexican rode up to the spot where Brent was aiming.

Brent squeezed the trigger slowly; his sight set on Lomax's chest. The hammer fell and made a dull thud. Brent's eyes widened as he quickly jacked that bad cartridge out and another one into the rifle's firing chamber.

He pulled the trigger and again the dull thud. Lomax was now passed the kill point and the other members of the gang blocked Brent's view of the leader. He'd missed his chance due to bad cartridges.

"Reloads," Brent said under his breath. "Lousy reloads."

Brent recalled having purchased several boxes of cartridges just before he and Julia had lit out for California and had joined up with the wagon train headed west. Lomax had escaped this time, but there'd be other chances.

"Lomax, I'm going to become your worst nightmare," Brent stated, making a pledge he fully intended on keeping.

Brent quickly ran to where he'd tied his horse and mounted up. He knew now what his next move would be. He was going to thwart everything this gang planned on doing. If they were going to rob a bank, train, stagecoach...anything whatsoever; he would be there to gum up the works. At least until he'd satisfied his blood lust against them.

Brent smiled as he thought of what his new role in life was now. He'd be a constant sore spot in Sam Lomax's life...a sore spot until he decided Lomax's time had run out...then he would kill him.

Lomax and his gang continued on towards Las Cruces unaware of how close they'd come to being involved in a shootout with one Brent Sackett. Lomax was totally focused on the job ahead of them. He would not only rob the bank in Las Cruces he would loot the entire town and then burn it down when they left. At least that was his plan.

Raymond D. Mason

Chapter
19

SAM LOMAX raised his hand and called the gang to a halt. He reined his horse around so he was facing all his men and began giving them their final orders before entering Las Cruces.

"I want you to break off in the teams we set up earlier. Ride on into Las Cruces and go the saloon you were assigned. I'll contact each team and let you know what you are supposed to do when I give you the word. Any questions," Lomax asked?

"You think we can really take over the whole town, Sam," one man asked?

"I know we can. The first thing we'll do is take the sheriff and his deputies out. The business owners are just that; business owners. They're not going to fight. Once we've got the law out of the way the town is ours for the taking," Lomax stated.

"And you'll tell us what you want us to do after the law is out of the way?" another man asked.

"That's right. I'll take care of the law, Boles and me. You boys will only do what I tell you after we've got the sheriff out of the way," Lomax reiterated.

When there were no more questions the men began to pair up and head on into Las Cruces. Lomax would time the teams of two, three, and four men and spaced them at four minute intervals. He and Billy Boles were the last to go.

Brent wanted to get good looks at the gang member's faces and would have to ride hard parallel to the trail in order to get ahead of them. He kicked his horse into a full run and made a half circle in order to get up ahead of them.

It was fortunate that the trail made a number of turns because it allowed Brent to get up ahead of the first two riders. Once he reached a spot that he could get back on the trail, he did so. He reined the horse around and headed back in the direction of the gang members.

Brent met the first two riders about two miles out of Las Cruces. He eyed the two men as they passed, as they did him. He rode on slowly. When he met the next three men he eyed them carefully, committing their faces to memory.

Brent reined his horse off the trail and stopped atop a slight rise behind some underbrush, well hidden from the sight of anyone on the trail. From here he would be able to see the men's faces as they passed but they would not be able to see him.

Finally Lomax and Boles made their appearance, and although he had never gotten a real good look at Lomax, Brent seemed to know he was the leader of the gang.

"Lomax," Brent said under his breath as Lomax passed.

He let Lomax and Boles get out of sight before he rode out from behind the underbrush and back onto the main trail. A wry grin pulled at the corners of Brent's mouth and he nodded his head with satisfaction as he knew what his next move would be now.

Brent kicked his horse into an easy lope and began following Lomax and Boles, but remaining at a safe distance behind them. Since Lomax didn't know that he was being followed it would be easy for Brent to keep a watchful eye on him without being noticed.

The anger of losing Julia to this bunch of cutthroats burned inside Brent. He wanted to see every one of the gang lying dead in the street. He'd alerted the sheriff, so with him behind the gang and the sheriff and his men ahead, they should be well prepared for Lomax and his gang.

Meanwhile, in Las Cruces, the sheriff had gathered together every able bodied man he could find and given them their orders and positioned them where he wanted them. The men were on rooftops, behind water barrels, inside businesses, and about five men in each of the two livery stables in town.

The sheriff and his three deputies handed out playing cards to each one of the men he'd deputized to be worn where they could be seen. He didn't want the townspeople shooting one another when the shooting started. They didn't have enough badges so the playing cards would act as such.

The sheriff and his men took positions across the street from the sheriff's office figuring that Lomax would come there first. They'd heard how gangs taking over towns had worked in the past and they weren't going to play by the gang's rules; not at all.

With the livery stables being at each end of town, a blockade could be set up quickly by pulling wagons loaded with hay into the road and when the gang tried to get away torch the hay, making it that much more difficult for them to escape. This idea had come from a retired Cavalry Officer by the name of Branch Rifkin.

Sam Lomax and Billy Boles rode down Las Cruces's main street looking left and right as they rode along. Lomax didn't like what he was seeing. There weren't a lot of people on the street or in the shops. He had an uneasy feeling about this and gave Boles a serious look.
"What do you think, Billy; what's your take on this?" Lomax asked.
"Looks like a lazy day in Las Cruces to me, Sam. This is the way most towns are in the middle of the week. The weekend is when folks hit the towns and shops."
"I hope you're right, but something smells fishy to me. Let's check on the men and make sure everyone is where they're supposed to be. I don't want any slip ups. Once we've checked on everyone and given them their orders, we'll take care of the sheriff," Lomax said, figuring he was just being a little overly cautious.
Brent Sackett rode a good two hundred yards behind Lomax and Boles. He watched the two men's every move as he followed unnoticed behind them. He looked forward to having a showdown with this bunch. His heart raced at the thought of the action that was about to take place.
When Lomax and Boles stopped in front of the first saloon they came to, 'Aces Wild', Brent rode to the side of the road and tied up at a hitching rail. He

waited until Lomax and Boles had entered the saloon before making his walk in that direction.

By the time Brent reached the saloon doors Lomax and Boles were coming out. The three of them met in the doorway and Lomax and Brent's eyes locked in a hard stare down.

Neither man spoke as they stood there staring at one another. Finally Lomax and Boles moved on to where their horses were tied. Brent looked around the room until he spotted the two men he'd first met on the trail as they rode into town. He knew instinctively that they were the two with whom Lomax had met.

Brent turned and watched Lomax and Boles ride on down the street to the next saloon. When they tied up in front of it, Brent knew that the saloons were where Lomax had his men positioned. Brent had no idea where the sheriff was, so he had no way of letting him know what he'd just figured out.

The sheriff had been watching Lomax's men riding into town through a hotel room window. He had wanted posters with him and was able to identify a number of the gang by their photos or descriptions. He also saw that Brent had returned.

The sheriff looked at his deputy and said, "That Brent Johnson; or whatever his name is; followed Lomax into the 'Aces Wild'. Lomax and the guy with him just came out and climbed aboard their horses and Johnson's watching them from the doorway of the Aces Wild," the sheriff said to the deputy who was in the room with him.

"You don't think that Johnson fella is part of the gang, do you?" the deputy asked.

"No, no...he warned me about Lomax and his gang coming this way. No, they're responsible for his wife's death. I just hope he doesn't go off half cocked and start shootin' it out with them.

"Now, Lomax is tying up in front of the Lazy Daze Saloon. It's my guess he's got men positioned in each of the saloons in town. Go down and have Bob George and those with him to get a fix on the ones Lomax talks to. If we can keep them bottled up in the saloons they can't join up for whatever it is they're planning to do," the sheriff ordered.

The deputy hurried out to pass the sheriff's orders along to the other special deputies. While he was busy doing that, the sheriff continued to watch Brent and saw him climb aboard his horse and ride down the street to the Lazy Daze Saloon.

Brent was doing exactly what the sheriff wanted his men to do; he was getting a fix on the men Lomax was contacting. As soon as he could, he planned on taking a number of the men out before the gang's plan could be carried out. By only a few men being scattered around in the various saloons, Brent would have a much easier time of gunning them down.

Brent entered The Lazy Daze Saloon and saw Lomax leaning over one of the tables talking to the two men who were seated there.

"Giving them their orders are you, Lomax?" Brent said under his breath.

When Lomax and Boles turned to leave, Brent turned and faced the bar. As they walked past him he heard Lomax say, "Now we'll go to the saloon near the bank."

Brent waited until they were outside and then gave the two men a good hard look that Lomax had just given their orders too. He remembered the short waist coat one of the men was wearing as being one of the ones shooting at the wagon when Julia was shot.

The man gave Brent a hard look which was the wrong thing to do at that time. Brent glared back at the man for several long seconds and when the man said, "What are you staring at?" Brent replied, "A dead man," and pulled his pistol and shot both men dead.

The entire saloon froze. Some men held drinks up to their mouth, but didn't drink. Men playing cards all turned their attention towards the gunfire; their mouths a gape.

Brent looked at the two men he'd just killed with a solemn look on his face. He turned and looked at those in the saloon and twirled his pistol on his index finger before holstering it.

"They tried to kill me," Brent said quietly as he turned and walked towards the saloon doors.

He turned and looked at the stunned onlookers and grinned, "I'll go tell the sheriff, so don't bother sending anyone."

The gunshots had not gone unnoticed by Lomax and Boles, but they just thought it was a couple of cowboys letting off steam. They were more convinced their assumption was right when they saw no one go running for the sheriff. All they saw was one man walk nonchalantly out of the saloon and climb aboard his horse.

Raymond D. Mason

Chapter
20

THE SHERIFF looked puzzled when he heard the gunshots. He was as much in the dark as to what had just happened in The Lazy Daze Saloon as Lomax and Boles were.

"I hope that wasn't who I think it might have been," the sheriff said to nobody seeing as how he was alone in the hotel room.

When he saw Brent casually walk out of the saloon he breathed a sigh of relief.

"Just a couple yahoos blowing off steam," he said.

Brent reloaded his revolver as he watched Lomax and Boles stop at another saloon a hundred yards away. Once they were inside Brent rode down the street and tied up next to their horses. He noticed their rifles in the saddle scabbard and looked to make sure he wasn't being observed.

Assured that no one was watching him he emptied the cartridges from the rifle on Lomax's horse, and then slid the gun back into the scabbard. He did the same with Boles' rifle. Once that was done he entered the saloon.

Looking around the crowded barroom, Brent saw Lomax and Boles talking to three men at a table in the back of the saloon. He went to the bar and ordered himself a beer. When the bartender took his order and went to get his drink, Brent looked behind the bar to see where they kept their shotgun. It was under the bar right at the spot where he was about to be served.

Lomax gave the three men their orders and started to go. When he noticed Brent he did a double take and gave him a stern look as he past by him on his way to the door.

Brent pretended not to notice Lomax, but it was all he could do to keep from gunning him down right then and there. He held back though, waiting for the right time to act out his revenge.

Lomax and Boles walked outside the saloon and Lomax stopped and looked back. Boles gave his leader a curious look and asked, "Is something wrong?"

Lomax didn't answer immediately, but after a couple of seconds said, "I don't know. Did you notice the guy standing at the bar near the door?"

"No, not really...why do you ask?" Boles questioned.

"I swear he was at the last saloon we were at. I have the feeling I've seen him somewhere before," Lomax stated.

"Maybe you're just getting a little jumpy about the job," Boles said causing Lomax to snap his head around in his direction.

"You know better than that. I've planned this thing out carefully and I don't want any mix ups. It might do you well to pay a little closer attention to what goes on around you, Boles."

"Hey, I didn't mean anything by it. I just hadn't noticed the man, that's all," Boles said quickly.

Lomax looked back down the street in the direction of the Lazy Daze. He saw the undertaker and a couple of other men rushing towards the saloon with a cart to haul off the bodies.

"I guess that was what those shots were about awhile back," Lomax said thoughtfully.

"I wonder who they were?" Boles questioned.

"Probably just a couple of waddies killing one another over some hussy," Lomax answered.

"Yeah," Boles agreed.

Meanwhile, inside the saloon they had just left, Brent was watching the three gang members seated at the table Lomax and Boles had just left. He waited until the bartender was at the other end of the bar and then leaned over the bar and grabbed the sawed off shotgun kept behind it.

Walking with the gun held down at his side, Brent made his way through the saloon without anyone noticing the shotgun. When he reached the table he stopped and before anyone knew what was happening, raised the shotgun and killed two of the gang members. Before the third could respond, Brent threw the gun and hit the man in the face with it while he pulled his pistol and shot the man dead.

Hearing the shotgun blast, Lomax and Boles rushed back into the saloon and saw Brent standing at the table where the three men had just been shot. They both pulled their pistols and opened fire in Brent's direction.

The first shot alerted Brent to the fact they had came back inside the saloon. He dived to the floor as the bullets passed dangerously close to his head. He returned fire; one, two, three shots. The second shot hit Boles in the shoulder. The other two missed.

Lomax jumped behind the bar. Brent began firing into the bar; the bullets passing right through the thin wooden veneer. Lomax felt the sting of hot lead in his leg and then again in his side. He grimaced in pain and looked for an escape route of some kind. He spotted a small sliding door where they kept a couple of extra beer kegs.

Quickly Lomax slid the door open and looked inside. There was only one keg of beer in the storage area, which allowed him plenty of room to take refuge in. He crawled inside and slid the door shut. He left just a crack in the door so he could watch one end of the bar.

Boles jumped up and ran for the saloon doors. He didn't make it. Brent pulled the second gun he kept in his boot top out and put a bullet between Boles' shoulder blades. He went down hard; never to get up again.

Now it was Lomax's turn. Brent moved to the far end of the bar; the end that was within Lomax's view. Brent slowly peered around the corner. When he didn't see Lomax he retreated out of the gang leader's view.

Brent moved down to the other end of the bar; the end that was hidden from Lomax's view. He knew that Lomax had not gotten away, so he had to be behind the bar somewhere.

Brent began to walk slowly behind the bar. When he saw the sliding door slightly ajar he knew that was where Lomax was hiding. Brent called out to Lomax as he reloaded his pistol.

"Come on out Lomax. I know you're hiding where they keep the extra beer kegs. Come out and face me like a man," Brent said angrily.

There was a moment of silence before Lomax finally answered back. His answer, however, was three gunshots. The wood splintered on the sliding door as the bullets passed through them. They didn't even come close to hitting Brent, however.

"Oh, you missed Lomax. Come on out. I want to see your face when I kill you," Brent said with a slight sneer.

"Who are you anyway? What did we ever do to you?" Lomax asked.

"You killed the only woman I've ever been in love with and you're going to die for it," Brent called back.

There was another moment of silence before Lomax answered, "Someone in the wagons?"

"You got it, Lomax. My wife was the woman you killed. Now come on out and face me. Either that or I'll start puttin' holes through that flimsy sliding door," Brent said, his words coming sharp and tight.

"I'll come out, but you've got to give me a chance," Lomax replied.

"I'll give you a chance. Like I said I want to see your face when I shoot you."

"I'm coming out," Lomax said.

The sliding door slowly began to slide open as Lomax cautiously stuck his head out to locate Brent's position. Then, instead of crawling out of the storage area head first, Lomax came out feet first; scooting himself out.

Brent had moved by the time Lomax was completely out of the beer storage area, and watched Lomax from around the end of the bar. He figured Lomax would try to get a quick shot at him once he knew his location...he was right.

127

Lomax had his gun in his hand and as soon as he saw Brent fired a quick shot that splintered wood at the end of the bar. Brent fired three shots; hitting Lomax in the chest or stomach. Lomax groaned loudly and curled up in a fetal position on the barroom floor.

Lomax's grip on the pistol he was holding slowly loosened as his life's blood drained out of him. Brent had killed Sam Lomax. Somehow the revenge wasn't as sweet as Brent had thought it would be. Lomax's death hadn't brought Julia back to him.

Brent stood up and looked down at the dead gang leader. The patrons who had been in the saloon when the shooting started had all run for cover, but now began to emerge from their hiding places surveying the barroom.

"That's Sam Lomax," someone said quietly.

"Are you sure?" someone else asked.

"Yeah I'm sure. Someone go and get the sheriff," the man said.

"I sent a man for him already," the bartender said.

Brent turned around and walked towards the saloon doors. When he got there he turned and gave one more look back at Lomax's body before walking outside to where his horse was tied.

By this time the sheriff and his deputies were beginning to round up some of the men they suspected of being members of the Lomax gang. Brent, however, rode out of town in the direction of Texas. He had a yearning in his heart to go home.

As he rode along his thoughts drifted back to Julia and in his mind's eye he saw a vision of her smiling face. A faint grin tugged at the corner of his lips and he whispered, "Julia...!"

Chapter
21

BRIAN AND AJ escorted Terrin and Homer to San Antonio without further incident. Timmons became more nervous, however, the closer they got to San Antonio. Brian noticed and made a comment to Miss Gibbons.

"Was this guy that nervous while you were being held captive by the Comancheros?"

"No. He acted timid, but I never had the feeling he was scared," Terrin replied.

"Well, he's certainly nervous and scared acting now. He's hiding something, you can be sure of that," Brent said and then gave Terrin a long admiring look.

"What are your plans now that you've called off your engagement?" Brian asked.

"I don't know. I'll have to think about what I want to do now. I really don't want to stay around here, though; I know that," Terrin replied.

"Isn't this where your family is though?" Brian questioned.

"Yes, some of them; we have a large family and they're scattered hither and yon," Terrin said with a smile.

"Do you have any kin up in the Taylor County area?" Brian asked with a slight grin.

Terrin looked at him with a surprised look and replied, "Why, yes I do. My sister and her husband live near Buffalo Gap."

"Are you kidding me? Why, our ranch isn't all that far from Buffalo Gap. There's a small settlement that we call Abilene, but it isn't formally a recognized town yet that's near Buffalo Gap. That's where our ranch is. Maybe you could come up that way and get your thoughts together...you know, in regards to what you want to do now that you've broken up with your fiancé," Brian said as he nervously tugged at his ear.

Terrin smiled warmly. The truth was that the first time she saw him she thought what a handsome man he was. It was obvious that he had eyes for her also.

"It has been a long time since I've visited my sister. I just might do that," Terrin said.

Brian beamed, "Here, let me give you our name and you could send a letter up and let me know when you're coming. In fact, if you wanted me to do so, I could come down and escort you up to your sister's place...you know, to make sure you got there safe."

"Oh, I wouldn't want to put you to all that trouble," Terrin smiled.

"No trouble at all," Brian grinned widely.

"Are you and AJ going to be in San Antonio for very long?" Terrin asked.

"Yeah, uh, no...actually we haven't made my...uh, our minds up yet," Brian said, fumbling his words.

Terrin smiled faintly.

"Uh, actually we haven't really decided what we're going to do yet. We have some business we have to get cleared up before we head back to our ranch, so I'm not sure how long that will take," Brian said gathering his thoughts together and sounding more decisive.

"Well, if you're going to be in town for awhile maybe we could have you and AJ out to our place for supper some night," Terrin offered.

"We'll be there...uh, whenever you invite us," Brian said jumping at the offer.

Just then AJ walked up to where they were standing and looked back towards Timmons.

"Boy... that Timmons is one nervous fella. I thought he was going to faint when the sheriff started asking him questions. He's doing a lot of talking, but not really saying a whole lot," AJ said with a grin; then noticing the looks passing between Brian and Terrin added, "I guess I barged in on something, huh?"

"Yeah...go water the horses," Brian said not taking his eyes off Terrin.

"I think I'll go water the horses," AJ said and laughed as he walked away.

"Well, I guess I'd better get back home and explain to the family about the breaking off of the engagement. Where are you and AJ going to be staying?" Terrin asked and then added. "You know, so I'll know where to reach you for the supper invitation?"

"Right over there at the hotel. We don't have a room yet, but we will," Brian smiled.

"Thank you for rescuing me from that bunch of cutthroats. I guess you are my knight in shining armor," Terrin said with a brilliant smile.

"I never saw myself as that," Brian said and scuffed the ground with the toe of his boot.

Terrin smiled again. She was taken by her 'knight in shining armor', that was evident. She turned and walked away, stopping when she passed AJ at the watering trough and thanked him as well for rescuing her and told him about the supper invitation that would be coming shortly.

Brian watched as Terrin climbed aboard the horse they had taken when they made their escape from the Comanchero's camp and rode away. AJ walked up to him, also looking over his shoulder and watching Terrin.

"Now there is the woman for you, little brother," AJ said seriously.

Brian didn't answer right away, but after collecting himself replied, "You've got that right."

The sheriff looked at AJ and Brian and nodded his head slowly. He opened his desk drawer and pulled out a folder filled with papers.

"See this," he said holding the folder out towards them, "I just received a number of these from the US marshal working the Del Rio area. There have been more charges filed against that crooked sheriff down there than you can shake a stick at. You boys merely did what the law would have eventually done.

"I don't think you have anything to worry about. Not from me, certainly. You're free to head on back up north to your ranch whenever you want to," the sheriff said.

"Man, is that good news," Brian said before adding, "Well, we might stick around here for a few days." He then asked, "When did you take over as sheriff here? The last time I went through here the sheriff was Roy LeBarge."

"Roy took a job as a US Marshal. The last I heard he was working up in the Colorado Territory. A good man, but don't cross him," the sheriff stated.

"I'll go along with that," Brian said. "Where's the best place in town to eat, Sheriff?" he then asked.

"The hotel; the one just down the street; they've got a fine restaurant, but you'll need a reservation. Everyone who is anyone in this town eats there," the sheriff stated.

"Come on, Brian," AJ said, "let's go make a reservation and sample this fine food. I'm starving."

"I'm right with you, AJ. Thanks for everything, Sheriff," Brian said as the two headed for the door.

The two men left the sheriff's office with a huge weight lifted off their shoulders. It didn't surprise them that Rawhide Deacon's brother was as crooked as a man could be. It must have been bad blood in the family line.

They went to the restaurant and found the place was completely full. The maitre' de told them it would be about a fifteen minute wait. They said they'd wait and Brian signed the reservation list with B. Sackett. They then went to the small bar off to one side to have a couple of drinks while they waited.

Ten minutes later a waiter came and told them their table was ready. He picked up their drinks and led them to their table. After giving him their orders they sat back to soak up the atmosphere.

Three men entered the restaurant and stopped at the maitre de's table. They all had a hard look about them. You could tell that they weren't comfortable in the business suits they wore. One of the men wore a suit that was a little tight on him.

AJ grinned slightly as he watched the three men. Brian noticed the grin and asked about it.

"What do you see that's so humorous?" he asked.

"Check those three out over by the door. You can tell they're out of their natural surroundings just by the way they're dressed," AJ said.

Brian looked their way and agreed, but with a side comment, "That's probably what the other patrons said about us when we walked in."

"You're more right than you know," AJ said with an agreeing nod.

The three men stood waiting for the maitre' de to seat them, but letting their eyes roam the large dining room. The older man, who looked to be the other men's father, glanced down at the reservation list to see how many names were ahead of theirs.

He stiffened when he saw the name Sackett with the first initial 'B'. He tapped the other two men on the shoulders and pointed to the name on the register. They all three began to scour the room with their gazes. When the older man's eyes fixed on Brian and AJ his face turned a slow red.

Brian and AJ frowned slightly when they saw the intense stare the man had trained on them. AJ looked at Brian and said quietly, "I wonder what that old fella's problem is?"

"I don't know, but it looks like he's concentrating on you," Brian replied.

"Me? Not me...I'd say you're the one he's taken a disliking to," AJ said with a chuckle.

The older man said something to the younger ones and they too cast long, hard stares in Brian and AJ's direction.

"Now the whole family is staring at us," AJ said and laughed.

The three men slowly began walking towards the Sackett brothers' table. The old man pushed his coat back so he could reach the big iron on his hip without any trouble.

"They're heading this way; be ready for what they might be bringing with them," AJ said seriously.

Brian pulled his pistol out and held it under the table where it was concealed by the large white table cloth. AJ did the same. The Rules approached the Sackett table cautiously.

"Which one of you is B. Sackett?" Earl Rule asked resting his hand on his pistol grip.

"I am, why?" Brian replied.

"My name is Earl Rule. Does that name mean anything to you?"

Brian shook his head negatively and said, "No, I don't recall ever hearing the name."

"Maybe the name Johnny Rule triggers a remembrance?" Earl said glaring at Brian.

Brian remembered that name. He knew then who the three men standing in front of him and AJ were. He'd been warned about the Rule family when Johnny Rule forced him into a showdown.

It was obvious what was about to happen here and Brian wanted no part of it. He cocked the hammer back on the pistol he held under the table; AJ did the same. The sound froze the Rules.

"I wouldn't do anything stupid if I was you," Brian said holding a steady gaze on Earl.

"That goes for you two boys as well," AJ said.

The Rules knew they had overplayed their hand and now they were the ones on the defensive. Earl glared at Brian and snapped angrily, "Johnny was my youngest and you took him from me."

"Look, Johnny forced me into a showdown and he drew down on me first. There were plenty of witnesses that saw exactly what happened. Unless I miss my guess you talked to all of them and some of them had to tell you what happened," Brian stated.

"You can't believe those lyin' good for nothings," Earl growled.

"So you did talk to them and they did tell you what happened. Look, Mr. Rule, I didn't want to have to kill your son, just like I don't want to kill you. But if it comes down to you or me...I'll do my best to make it you. All three of you if need be," Brian said evenly.

"I'll not let you gun down my other two sons in cold blood like you did Johnny, but we'll be seeing you again, both of you. You'll not leave San Antone alive," Earl Rule said with clenched teeth.

"I suggest you turn around and walk out of here right now," Brian said.

Earl looked at Brian and then turned and gave AJ the same hate filled look. He glanced quickly at his two boys and snapped, "Come on...let's go. We'll eat out of a pig sty with the pigs before I'll eat in the same restaurant with these two."

The three Rules turned and walked towards the door. Brian gave AJ a quick look and said, "Move."

The two of them moved quickly apart; Brian to his left and AJ to his right. They were a good ten feet from where they had been seated when the Rules spun around and went for their guns.

When they turned back to open fire on Brian and AJ they were slightly shocked to see nothing but an empty table. By the time they spotted AJ and Brian it was too late.

Guns started blazing. First, Cory Rule fired at the empty chair where he thought Brian would still be sitting. Brian's shot hit Cory in the forearm, shattering the bone and bringing a cry of pain from the youngest Rule while sending his gun flying a good six feet away from him.

Rupert's shot barely missed AJ, but AJ's hit Rupert in the rib cage, taking him to the floor. Earl fired quickly at Brian, but missed. Brian fired two quick shots that hit Earl in the hip and thigh. Earl fell hard to the floor and hit his head on a chair on the way down. The blow knocked him out.

Cory and Rupert were moaning loudly as they lay writhing on the floor. Earl was out like a light, so he would be causing no trouble until he woke up and that would probably be in jail.

Brian walked over to Cory and looked down at him, "You'll be all right. Quit your howling."

He then walked over to Rupert and checked his wound and said," You ain't going to die. Count your blessings."

AJ and Brian stayed with the wounded Rules until the sheriff arrived and had them all three hauled off to the doctors office to be patched up. Once that was taken care of he looked at Brian and AJ and said, "I'll hold them for three days. You boys be gone when the three days run out."

Raymond D. Mason

Chapter
22

BRENT SACKETT made camp about thirty minutes before the sun disappeared behind a distant range of mountains. He built a fire and was warming a can of beans; his mind locked on the memory of Julia.

He sat staring into the fire and remembering the color of her hair and the way she tilted her head when he said something for her to ponder. He loved the lilt of her laughter and the way her eyes would crinkle up when she smiled.

As he peered into the flames it was almost as if he could see her peering back at him. The thought was so overwhelming it almost took his breath away. He sat straight up, afraid to blink for fear of losing her image.

A thought so strong he could have sworn it was actually speaking to him in Julia's voice said, "They need you, Brent."

He shook his head and blinked. The vision went away, but the thought remained...'they need you'. Had he just had a vision of Julia and she was telling him to go back because the ones he'd left in Las Cruces needed him; or what?

Brent looked around him as if expecting to see someone there. The thought and vision were so real that they left him somewhat confused. He knew his life had changed from the moment he met Julia, but this was something altogether different. He'd had that connection with Brian before, but now it was with Julia...and she was dead.

Brent began to think of the Thurston kids and Grant Holt and little Gracie, Grant's baby. Julia was telling him they needed him. But, she was doing it from the grave!

Suddenly Brent was overwhelmed with a kind of sadness unlike anything he had ever experienced. It wasn't like the sadness he was experiencing over the loss of Julia; this was sadness over the plight of the Thurston kids and Grant. They were totally alone in the world now.

A growing sense of urgency began to build inside of Brent as he tried to fight off the feelings and the thoughts. No matter how hard he tried, however, he could not shake that feeling; and it disturbed him greatly.

"I can't go on to California without you...I miss you too much. Being out there without you would be like being stuck between heaven and hell," Brent said aloud as he looked up into the darkening sky.

He slowly lowered his head and closed his eyes. He held his head down for several long seconds and finally nodded it as if getting orders of what he should do.

"Okay...okay; I will," he said as tears filled his eyes.

Brent slept better that night than he had for weeks. When he awoke in the morning he fixed himself a quick bite to eat and then broke camp and headed back to Las Cruces.

It didn't take him long to make the trip back into town, but when he got there he could find no one who knew what had happened to Grant Holt and his baby girl, or the Thurston kids. No one even remembered Dobbs.

Brent rode to the livery stable that was on the west end of Las Cruces and saw his and Julia's wagon sitting beside the corral. There were no horses hitched to it, and his first thought was that Grant had sold the wagon to the stable owner.

When Brent rode up next to the wagon he heard Grant talking to the Thurston kids. He was explaining to them that they wouldn't have to worry; he'd make sure they had a place to live. A grin tugged at both Brent's mouth...and his heart.

He stepped down off his horse and tied the bridle reins to the wagon wheel. Slowly he walked around to the back of the wagon and peeked around the canvas covering.

When Annie Thurston saw Brent peering in at them her eyes widened and she pointed and yelled excitedly, "Brent!"

Grant and Hank snapped their heads around and looked at Brent. At first none of them spoke, but then Brent said, "Is anyone here going to California?"

With those words wide grins broke out on the faces of Grant and Hank. Annie was already smiling, but she giggled. Brent pushed the canvas back a little more.

"I think we'd better pick up a few supplies before we strike out again, don't you Grant?" Brent said with a half grin.

Grant let out a laugh and slapped his leg, "You said it, Brent. California here we come."

"California here we come," Annie Thurston said.

Hank Thurston looked at his sister and then burst into laughter himself as he said, "California here we come."

Earl Rule sat in a San Antonio jail cell nursing a sore head and wounds to his hip and thigh. His mood was more sour than usual, but he remained quiet due to the pain in his head whenever he raised his voice above a whisper.

His boys, Rupert and Cory were in the cell next to him, also with bandages covering their wounds. Neither boy wanted to carry this vendetta any further than it had gone, but they knew better than to cross their pa.

The sheriff walked to the jail cell door and looked in at Earl Rule. He stood there for several seconds before finally speaking.

"Earl I'll let you and your boys out of here as soon as the doctor says you can go. He figures it to be in a couple of days. I want this thing with Sacketts to end right here."

"It'll end when either Brian Sackett or I are dead and not before," Earl Rule said solemnly.

"I don't want any shooting in San Antone, do you hear me. You take your hate out of town. There was a room full of innocent folks in the restaurant last night that could have been hurt or even killed. If it happens again you'll have me to deal with; do you hear me?"

"I hear you. Like I said, this thing with Sackett will be over when I see him in his grave," Rule said.

"This is all over the death of your youngest son, Johnny, from what I've heard. You almost got your other two boys killed last night, as well as yourself.

Isn't one death in your family enough," the sheriff asked with a deep frown.

Earl Rule didn't answer nor did his expression change. Hatred had a permanent home in Earl's heart. He wallowed in hatred like pigs wallow in mud. It was rumored he had killed his wife in a fit of jealous rage several years before, but there was no way of proving it. His sons certainly hadn't come forth with any information. They feared him as much, if not more, than other people did.

All the sheriff could do was to keep him and Brian Sackett apart temporarily. Once he let the Rules out it was out of his hands until they broke the law. He just hoped the Sackett boys heeded his advice and left town.

Raymond D. Mason

Chapter 23

Las Cruces, New Mexico

BRENT SACKETT sat astraddle his horse and looked back at Grant Holt as he climbed aboard the wagon and took the harness reins in preparation of continuing their trek to California. The Thurston kids sat on the wagon seat with Grant. Dobbs sat hunched over slightly holding the harness reins and Mrs. Keeling who was seated next to him on the wagon, held little Gracie.

"Let's go to California," Brent said with a slight grin.

Brent took the lead and they struck out again. There was a sense of caring in Brent's heart now. He truly felt a concern for the Thurston kids and for Grant and little Gracie.

This is not the way of life Brent had figured on living, but after having loved Julia the way he had, it seemed right. He had no idea what their life would be like in California, but he knew it would be an adventure.

Dobbs had every chance to turn him in and hadn't, so he now felt he could trust the man; within reason. Dobbs was a gambler and it was hard to figure a gambler's next move.

They left Las Cruces around six o'clock in the morning hoping to cover fifteen to twenty miles. There was a small settlement about fifty miles away. There wasn't much there, but they would be able to pick up any additional supplies they might need.

From there it would be another three to four day journey to Lordsburg. Brent had laid their stops out on a map he'd gotten when they first started the trip to California. Hopefully there would be good water along the way.

There was an overall good feeling among everyone. Even Dobbs had lost some of his sharp edges. He was much easier going with the kids; something for which they were both grateful.

Brent rode ahead of the wagons; his mind drifting back to Julia. The sense of loss was strong, but when he'd look at the Thurston kids and Grant and his baby, he felt better. Julia had cared so much for them all.

He was the head of a 'family' whether he wanted to be or not. His heart had softened to a point that there was more love in it now than hate; thanks to Julia. She had been responsible for so many changes in his life.

Whatever lay ahead of them they'd face together and would probably grow even closer. He could already see how Annie Thurston would want to be near him in the evening, much like a little girl does her father. In the beginning it had been Hank she would cling to.

Brent was so thankful that Mrs. Keeling had decided to go on to California with them since she had family already out there. She had taken to little Gracie much the same way Julia had.

Mrs. Keeling told Brent that she had informed the sheriff of how the man named Manny Chavez had helped her and Dobbs escape. It was the sheriff that informed her that Chavez was a Texas Ranger. Chavez had actually helped the sheriff and his deputies capture most of the gang.

Brent looked back as they passed by the city limit sign and felt that sense of adventure again. The trail was fairly easy going through these parts. There would be some rough spots, but they'd make it. Brent was sure of that.

San Antonio, Texas

Terrin Gibbons had left an invitation to supper at the hotel's front desk, along with directions of how to find her family's place. Brian and AJ rode out to the small farm and tied up in front of the house.

Brian knocked on the door and was greeted by Terrin. She smiled warmly at both Brian and AJ and then looked back at Brian with yet another warm grin. He smiled and cast a quick glance at AJ who was grinning like a Cheshire cat.

"I'm so glad you made it. My folks are dying to meet you both," she said.

"We're looking forward to meeting them also," Brian said.

"I hope you like chicken, because that's what we're having for supper," Terrin said.

"As long as the feathers are off of it," Brian joked.

"Oh, brother," AJ said as he rolled his eyes. "You are one sweet talker, I must say."

Brian gave him a quick frown and followed Terrin into the house. AJ followed and chuckled lightly at Brian's agitation. The Gibbons were pleased to meet the ones who had freed their daughter from the Comancheros.

They had supper and then adjourned to the living room to have their coffee. Mr. Gibbons wanted to know all about their ranch. He was looking at raising some cattle, mainly for their own benefit. AJ did most of the talking to him, while Brian and Terrin made constant eye contact.

There was definitely an attraction between Brian and Terrin. It had been like he had always thought it would be when he met the right woman. He was thinking more and more that she just might be 'the right one for him'. She was thinking the same thing.

Mrs. Gibbons noticed the looks passing between Brian and Terrin and smiled knowingly. She watched as Terrin would sneak glances in Brian's direction and was aware of his doing the same. In order to give the two a chance to be alone, she suggested that Terrin show Brian the new foal they had.

"I'm sure Brian would like to see that fine little strawberry roan that was born last week, Terrin. Why don't you take him out to the barn and show him?" Mrs. Gibbons suggested.

Terrin jumped at the chance. Because it was getting dark, Terrin grabbed an oil lantern and the two of them walked out to the barn. They walked up to the stall where the week old foal was being kept and Brian smiled as he looked at the colt.

"That's a fine looking little animal. Is he yours?" Brian asked.

"Yes, Papa said I could have him. Of course, he said he would break him to ride," Terrin stated.

The two of them eyed the horse for a few moments and then Brian looked down into Terrin's eyes. They gazed at one another for a moment and then Brian leaned forward and kissed her soft, yielding lips.

When their lips parted Brian said, "When can you get up to Buffalo Gap to visit your sister?"

"Not until next month," Terrin said quickly.

"I'll need directions to your sister's place. I want you to meet my family, too," Brian said with a slight grin. "Will you be coming up by stagecoach?"

"Yes, I've made the trip a number of times and it's rather a pleasant journey," Terrin replied.

"I'll need the date you're planning on leaving because I want to meet the stage when it gets to Buffalo Gap."

"I'll let you know before you leave tonight," Terrin said as she continued to gaze up into his eyes.

They kissed again tenderly. They both knew that something special was taking place. Due to the ordeal with the Comancheros there was already a strong bond between the two. Terrin felt safe in Brian's company and he felt protective of her.

When they returned to the house she gave him a definite date that she would be leaving on the trip north. Her mother and father gave each other a knowing glance, but didn't comment. They liked both the Sackett boys and sensed they came from a good, solid family.

Brian told them they would stop by the next day and say goodbye since they would be heading back to their ranch. They said their goodnight and headed back into San Antonio to their hotel.

"Looks like you may have met the right one, Brian," AJ said as they rode away from the Gibbons farm.

"It certainly looks and feels that way to me," Brian said.

"She comes from good stock," AJ said seriously.

Brian looked over at his brother and said, "I'm not buying livestock, AJ. That is the woman I plan on marrying back there."

AJ laughed, "I know, I know. I could hear wedding bells the moment you laid eyes on her. She's a keeper, I'll say that."

"Now you've gone fishing," Brian said, and then under his breath said, "keeper!"

Chapter 24

**Five miles out of
Las Cruces, NM**

BRENT SACKETT was about a mile and a half ahead of the wagons when he saw the two riders off to his left as the men topped a distant hilltop. They were heading in his direction. Brent reined his horse up and pulled his pistol from his holster, holding it down at his side so it was hidden from the approaching riders view.

If they were men on the run they might be in need of some cash or supplies and try and get it from them. They rode up to where Brent was and stopped. Instantly Brent recognized one of the men. He was a hired gun from Crystal City, Texas.

"Howdy," the man Brent knew as Red Harper said with a grin.

"Howdy," Brent replied in a deep voice.

"We saw the wagons back behind you from the ridge up there. Where you folks headed?" Harper asked.

"For California," Brent said, wondering if Harper would recognize him.

"We're on our way to Socorro. You haven't seen any other riders along here have you?" Harper asked.

"No, I haven't…why?" Brent questioned.

"We're supposed to meet up with a couple more men who are heading up that way. We're going to work for a big rancher up there," Harper said and then gave Brent a curious look. "Say, don't I know you?"

"I doubt it. Are you from Kansas?" Brent replied.

"Ain't ever been there," Harper said.

Brent still had a good growth of beard and that was probably why Harper couldn't recall his name.

"What's going on up Socorro way?" Brent asked curiously and wanting to change the subject.

"There's a feud about to boil over and we've been hired to help one of the ranchers out," Harper said still eyeing Brent curiously.

"There's never a winner in a range war. Even the winner comes out loser," Brent said.

Harper nodded his head in agreement and said, "Well the ones who get paid come out all right."

"If they live to spend the money," Brent grinned.

Harper shook his head, "Man you sure seem familiar to me."

"I have a common face I guess," Brent said with a frown.

Just then the other man spoke up, "Hey, Red. Look up there. Isn't that three men on horseback."

Red and Brent both looked in the direction off to the right and saw three riders atop a ridge about a mile away.

"That's them," Red said and then looked at Brent as he kicked his horse up, "Adios stranger. Good luck in California."

"Good luck in Socorro," Brent called after the two as they rode off to catch up to the three riders on the ridge.

Brent had dodged a bullet, so to speak. Now he wondered if he'd ever really be able to run far enough to be freed from his past. Hopefully things would be better in California. Only time would tell. Until then he'd keep trying to find his way to the life he and Julia had hoped for, only it would have to be without her now.

San Antonio, Texas

Brian and AJ checked out of the hotel and headed north. They planned on stopping by the Gibbons place to say goodbye and then back to the ranch.

Meanwhile, in the San Antonio jailhouse, Earl Rule had struck up a conversation with a man the sheriff was holding until he could get some information on him...Homer Timmons. It seems the sheriff did have a telegram to hold him until a positive identification could be made of him.

"You said you want to kill Brian Sackett, right? I can tell you where his ranch is; but, you have to get me out of this jail," Timmons said.

"You know where the Sackett ranch is?" Rule questioned, glaring at Timmons out from under bushy eyebrows.

"I heard him tell the Gibbons woman. You get me out of here and I'll tell you," Timmons said.

"Tell me now," Earl snapped.

"No, if I do you might not get me out of here. No, you get me out and then I'll tell you."

"I'll get you out, but you'd better not be lying to me or you'll be leaving jail and headed for Boot Hill," Earl growled.

"I know where they hang their hats, believe me," Timmons said confidently.

"Okay, it's a deal. When do you want us to spring you?" Earl asked.

"As soon as you can...I have to be out of here before an inspector from the bank arrives. He should be here in about two days."

"We get out tomorrow. We'll get you out of here tomorrow night," Earl Rule said evenly.

Timmons grinned. This would be payback for the Sacketts being responsible for his being held in jail for questioning. He'd be more than glad to point the Rules in the direction of the Sackett ranch.

Earl Rule lay back on his cot and looked up at the ceiling. He would go to the ends of the earth to see Brian Sackett dead. A grin forced its way into the naturally down turned mouth of Earl Rule.

"We shall meet again, Brian Sackett," he said under his breath.

The End

Look for the next book in 'The Sackett Series' (Book #7):
"Guns of Vengeance Valley"

Other books in the Sackett series are:
Across the Rio Grande
Three Days to Sundown
Ride the Hard Land
Range War
Five Faces West
Other series by this author you might enjoy:
Durango Series
Streets of Durango: The Lynching
Streets of Durango: The Shooting
Quirt Adams Series
The Long Ride Back (Quirt Adams #1)
Return to Cutter's Creek (Quirt Adams #2)
Ride the Hellfire Trail (Quirt Adams #3)
Brimstone: End of the Trail (Quirt Adams #4)
Night Riders (Quirt Adams #5)
Luke Sanders Series
Day of the Rawhiders
Moon Stalker
Westerns
Aces and Eights (Dead Man's Hand)
Beyond the Great Divide
Beyond the Picket Wire
Four Corners Woman
Incident at Medicine Bow
Laramie
Last of the Long Riders
Night of the Blood Red Moon
Rage at Del Rio
Rebel Pride
Showdown at Lone Pine
Tales of Old Arizona
The Man from Silver City
Yellow Sky, Black Hawk

Raymond D. Mason

Mysteries
Dan Wilder Series (Humorous)
A Walk on the 'Wilder' Side
Send in the Clones
Murder on the Oregon Express
A Tale of Tri-Cities
Odor in the Court
Frank Corrigan Series
Corrigan
Shadows of Doubt
The Return of Booger Doyle
Nick Castle Series
Brotherhood of the Cobra
Beyond Missing
Suddenly, Murder
Rick Russell Series
The Mystery of Myrtle Creek
If Looks Could Kill
Also:
8 Seconds to Glory
A Motive for Murder
Blossoms in the Dust
Counterfeit Elvis (Welcome to My World)
Illegal Crossing
In the Chill of the Night
Most Deadly Intentions
On a Lonely Mountain Road
Sleazy Come, Sleazy Go
The Mystery of Myrtle Creek
The Secret of Spirit Mountain
The Tootsie Pop Kid
The Woman in the Field
Too Late to Live

Between Heaven and Hell

Raymond D. Mason

6

Printed in Great Britain
by Amazon